ONE
CYCLE

A PODIUM SPORTS ACADEMY BOOK

LORNA SCHULTZ
NICHOLSON

JAMES LORIMER & COMPANY LTD., PUBLISHERS
TORONTO

James Lorimer & Company Ltd., Publishers acknowledges the support of the
Ontario Arts Council. We acknowledge the financial support of the Government
of Canada through the Canada Book Fund for our publishing activities. We
acknowledge the support of the Canada Council for the Arts which last year
invested $24.3 million in writing and publishing throughout Canada. We acknow-
ledge the Government of Ontario through the Ontario Media Development
Corporation's Ontario Book Initiative.

Library and Archives Canada Cataloguing in Publication

Schultz Nicholson, Lorna
    One cycle / Lorna Schultz Nicholson.

(A Podium Sports Academy book)
Issued also in an electronic format.
ISBN 978-1-4594-0184-6 (bound).--ISBN 978-1-4594-0183-9 (pbk.)

    I. Title. II. Series: Schultz Nicholson, Lorna. Podium Sports
Academy.

PS8637.C58O64 2012   jC813'.6   C2012-903694-3

James Lorimer & Company Ltd.,   Distributed in the United States by:
Publishers   Orca Book Publishers
317 Adelaide Street West, Suite 1002   P.O. Box 468
Toronto, ON, Canada   Custer, WA USA
M5V 1P9   98240-0468
www.lorimer.ca

Printed and bound in Canada.

Manufactured by Friesens Corporation in Altona, Manitoba, Canada in August 2012.
Job #77086

CHAPTER ONE

My thigh muscles screamed in pain. I sprinted down the field, holding my lacrosse stick at my shoulders, hoping for that perfect pass. When I saw the ball flying toward me, I snagged it from the air without breaking stride. I cradled my stick to keep possession of the ball. As an attack player, my mission was to get to the net and fire the hard lacrosse ball past the goalie. And I knew he could be beaten on his right top corner.

But first I had to get by the defenders. And they were big. Like massive. Most had 50 to 90 pounds on me. At five foot ten and 125 pounds, I wasn't exactly a heavyweight.

A defender with arms as big as my legs barrelled toward me, and I knew he wanted to slam me to the ground before I could take my shot. He waved his stick at me, ready to slash my forearms, hands, legs, any body part that would make me lose the ball. In a quick split dodge, I darted around him. Then I scanned the net. That top corner was open and if I could nail it, we would win. Only minutes remained in the game.

I whipped my stick back behind my head to use

momentum and all my muscles to shoot. Just as I was about to fire the ball, a second defender blindsided me with a slide tackle bodycheck. My feet went out from under me and I tumbled like a paper sack with nothing in it. I swear I did two somersaults before landing with a thud on the ground. My shoulder cracked. My head pounded. Stars swam in front of my face.

From my years of training, my entire body automatically curled. I rolled a few times before I bounced back onto my feet. Immediately I checked the field to see where the ball had landed. By now my fellow teammate, Quinn Hamilton, who had given me the perfect pass and played on my attack line, was in a battle with the opposing defenders. At six foot two, Hambone, as I called him, was four inches taller than me and seventy pounds heavier.

Sticks smacked against each other as at least four players tried to pick up the now-loose ball. Crap. I had lost possession.

I ran toward the scrum. My body ached from the hit, but I understood pain and had to play through it. Often I finished a game battered and bruised, and on the field was not the time to think about what hurt. I pushed into the group of players and poked my stick toward the ball to scoop it up, or free it so one of my teammates could get it. The big bodies knocked me sideways but I went at them again. Again I was tossed aside. And again I went back at them, grunting with every move. Then I saw the free ball.

Quick as I could, I ducked under the bodies and stuck my stick out to push the ball to Hambone. But I got caught and was slammed in the jaw. I had grown five inches in the past six months and was playing like an awkward giraffe.

"Cover him!" the defender yelled.

They had my number. They knew I played scrappy lacrosse, so I was shoved backwards onto my butt. In the time it took me to get up — which was only a half second at best — the defender from the other team had picked up the ball and made a quick pass down the field to his midfielder, who was now running full tilt.

The momentum had changed.

And it was my fault.

I took off running and chasing, and every step was painful. Time wasn't on our side now. The reversed play was my mistake. If they scored, they would win and I couldn't let that happen. I pushed, taking longer and longer strides, and overtook one guy, then two. Running was my best strength. I could do it.

Come on, Nathan. Keep going. No pain, no gain.

I was halfway down the field when the whistle blew to end the game. I came to a crashing halt, and my first emotion was relief that they hadn't scored. I slowed to a walk. I was still breathing heavy, and the lactic acid in my leg muscles made them ache. I slammed my stick on the ground.

A 4–4 tie. What a brutal outcome.

I gritted my teeth. If I'd scored, we would have won the game. How could I have lost possession like that? How could I have let someone blindside me that way? I hated it when I made mistakes, when I was the guy who didn't get the job done. As the captain of the team, I needed to show leadership and I needed to score goals.

A win would have put us first in our pool. But a tie, because of points for and against, put us second. Now for the semifinal game, we were matched up against a team that was higher ranked, more difficult to beat. Coming first would've almost given us a guaranteed berth in the finals, because the team we would've had to play had snuck in and was junk.

I lowered my head as I walked toward our bench. I didn't want to look at the fans; I didn't want to see the scouts, in their college jackets, watching the game. I knew they were there. This annual tournament in Baltimore was the biggest National Collegiate Athletic Association (NCAA) and professional lacrosse scouting tournament of the fall season. Our season really started in the spring, but in the fall we played tournaments for exposure.

At the sidelines our coach, Derkie — short for Joe Derkson — said, "I'll meet you in the dressing room. No one leave."

As captain I knew I should say something positive to my teammates, but the words stuck in my throat. I plodded off the field toward the dressing room, my feet feeling as if they each weighed a million pounds. Hambone walked quietly beside me. After we had walked almost halfway without talking, he said, "You got rocked."

"I know," I replied without looking at him. Hambone was one of those brutally honest dudes who told it like it was. To me he was like a dog with a bone, thus the nickname. "Really rocked. I didn't even get a shot on net."

"Don't kill yourself. The guy's gotta weigh in at 230."

"We coulda won if I'd scored." I walked a few strides

before I mumbled, "Thanks for the pass."

"We're not out."

"Yeah."

"I saw the scout from Syracuse."

"Yeah," I mumbled again. Then I whispered more to myself than to Hambone, "He probably just knocked me off his list."

Our team had travelled from Podium Sports Academy in Calgary to a big field lacrosse tournament in Baltimore. Podium was *the* national sports school in Canada and you had to be invited to attend. I had received my letter in the mail before grade ten, and the training and skills I had received so far were unbelievable. My game had improved a hundred percent. Podium is such a natural feeder school for getting NCAA college scholarships. And here I was at the top tourney, desperately needing a scholarship to keep playing my sport, and sucking because I was built like a stick. There was no way I was ready to quit playing lacrosse yet, but after today . . . was the writing on the wall?

No. Stop thinking like that. You've got the height, you just need the weight.

I had big dreams. But I was skinny, and the guys chirped me about it all the time. And yes, the comments bugged me but I made like they didn't. Fact was, I needed time to fill out before I even *thought* about playing professional box lacrosse — that means in an arena, like a hockey rink — in the National Lacrosse League. And that was my ultimate goal. So I had to get a scholarship to a Division 1 school to give me that time. At five-ten and 125 pounds I needed muscle. But my dad was skinny too, tall and lean and a runner. I had a runner's build, not a pro lacrosse athlete's build. Had I been born into a bad gene pool?

No. Stop thinking like that. You can build muscle.

I clenched my stick. I didn't have a hope of playing box lacrosse if I couldn't play field. And I didn't have tons of time to gain the muscle. I needed it now. I hadn't thought that with field lacrosse, my size would be a big factor — until today. I had been tossed around. I couldn't let Blackie — Jonah Black, our team trainer — know how much I was hurting from the hits. A sports medicine student, Blackie gave us ice, wrapped our legs with tensors, massaged our muscles, fixed cuts with butterfly bandages, and was an awesome sounding board for anything you wanted to talk about. But if you complained about an ache, he was quick to refer you to the right doctor, and that usually meant some time off — which I didn't want.

Hambone and I entered the dressing room. I went straight to my stall and tossed my stick on the floor and my helmet in the bag. I plopped down, took off my soaking wet headband, leaned my head against the wall, and closed my eyes. My hair hung in wet strands over my face. I still had tomorrow. I had to make up what was lost.

I'd spent a lot of time drafting the letter I sent to every lacrosse coach of the colleges I wanted to attend, making sure they all knew I was going to be playing in Baltimore. I'd also sent off a video that had taken hours to edit. It showed me performing all kinds of skills, playing well in games, and *scoring goals.* Today I didn't get one flipping point.

I moaned. All that work, just to be bounced around like a ping pong ball.

The door creaked and Derkie walked in the dressing room.

"Tough tie," he said, looking around the room. "But we're not out." His gaze rested on me. I wanted to lower my head but knew if I did, Derkie would definitely single me out. One of his pet peeves was a guy who couldn't hold his head up after a defeat. At the beginning of the year he had called me into his office and made me captain because he said he thought I was the most skilled player, had the right stuff to be a leader, plus I was someone who could stand up and handle every single situation with a positive attitude. Today I wasn't exactly doing that.

"We can win this tournament," said Derkie. "But everyone has to stay positive. We're a team and we work as a team to win, lose, and . . . tie." He broke our gaze and once again looked around the room, making eye contact with every other player, one after the other. I felt my shoulders sag. He was right. I had to stop acting like I was a one-man team and thinking only of my own scholarship.

Derkie continued. "It's very doable. I want to meet for an early breakfast tomorrow to go over some plays. We need to work on our attack. Goals win games. Our defence was solid and netminding was good, but I have some ideas on how we can push through *their* defence. I have a room booked in the hotel and will send a message about time later. Now get showered. We have a team meal in an hour."

After Derkie left, I stood up. "Derkie's right," I said loudly. "We *will* win tomorrow. Let's stay focused and positive and work as a team to take home the gold." I looked at my teammates. They had played hard. I had let them down. I grinned because I knew the guys expected me to be upbeat. "We didn't come all the way from Can-a-da to crap the bed."

Everyone in the room cheered and I nodded my head in reassurance. Then I undressed, wrapped my towel around my waist, and entered the shower.

As I stood there, water pouring over my body, I was still pissed off at myself. I had to get over it though, and now was the best time. Ryan Duncan stood beside me, shampooing his hair. He was a massive dude, and one of our best defencemen.

"Bro, you need some bulk," he said, his head back, eyes closed, as he shampooed his hair. "Your breastbone damn near hits your spine." He paused for a moment, then rolled his head to the side and opened one eye. "I know where you can get it."

"Oh yeah?" A little voice in my head told me to get showered and fast. But instead I took my time, even though my stomach had tightened. Maybe I should hear him out.

"Guy works at Rocky's Supplement Store," said Ryan, just loud enough for me to hear. "He knows tons." He shut his eyes again and stuck his head under the shower to rinse off the shampoo.

I thought about his comment. "Protein stuff?"

"Better."

"Creatine?"

He grinned and winked. "Better than that."

I shook my head. "My dad's a doc. He'd freak."

Ryan shrugged, then scrubbed his armpits, casually creating lather and bulging biceps at the same time. "It's your career. Not his."

I turned off the taps, wrapped my towel around my waist, and left the shower area, my mind racing. It wasn't like I hadn't thought about doing something, anything, to get bigger. Other guys did stuff all the time; it wasn't a secret in the sports world. But I was cursed with a father who was a doctor and who'd told me over and over how harmful steroid use was.

I approached my stall. Hambone had finished his shower and was getting dressed. "I'm *starving*," I said to him.

"I'd love a steak," he replied with a moan.

"Think again, dude. Five bucks says it'll be pasta." I quickly dressed in my game suit, leaned over, and shook my head to dry my long mop of hair, picked up my bag, and headed toward the door. "See you on the bus!" I yelled over my shoulder.

Once outside, I sucked in a deep breath because I saw Derkie talking to a man in a Syracuse jacket. As soon as Derkie saw me, he gestured at me to come over.

Crap. Crap. Crap. Why today?

I ran my hand through my hair, wishing I'd dried it with the dryer, squared my shoulders, and walked toward the duo. *Make eye contact. Be confident.* I stuck my hand out first. "Nathan Moore," I said.

The man returned the handshake. "John Markham. Pleased to meet you, Nathan."

"Likewise," I replied.

Derkie placed his hand on my shoulder. "I'll leave you

two to chat." Then he looked at his watch. "Bus leaves in ten," he said.

Mr. Markham gave a perfunctory nod and smiled, and I knew he was trying to make me relax. Once Derkie was out of earshot, he said, "He runs a tight ship."

"Yeah," I replied. "He sure does."

"I know we only have a few minutes today," said Mr. Markham, "so we have to be quick. But I wanted to touch base with you."

I gave him a small nod. My mouth had dried instantly, and my palms had started to sweat. "Quick" was not a good thing. At least I thought it wasn't. Something punched my gut and I swear my stomach flipped ten times.

"I like how you play," he said. "I like your heart and Derkie has said great things about your drive and passion. I'm always looking for that in a player."

"Thanks." I made sure I was holding on to the eye contact. Was this going better than I'd thought?

"But you need some weight to be an effective player."

My heart thudded to my toes. It was always the same comment. Although it used to be I was too small; now I was just too skinny. I swallowed. My lips were so dry but I didn't dare lick them. I couldn't let him see my disappointment.

"I'm working out with weights," I said, hoping I sounded confident.

"That's what Derkie said. He also said you are his hardest worker in the gym. To me, that's important. Keep it up." Then he stuck out his hand again. "You'll get there. I will definitely be looking at you in the next six months. You've got the talent, Nathan, and the drive and passion. With a little bulk, you'll go far." He reached out his hand and I shook it hard.

"I'll be at your game tomorrow."

"Great," I replied.

CHAPTER TWO

"So how did it *really* go this weekend?" Allie asked.

We sat beside each other on the sofa in the basement rec room, watching an episode of *Two and a Half Men*. Her long legs were casually looped over mine, our hips and shoulders glued together. All I wanted to do was feel her, touch her, run my hands all over her amazingly taut body. I stroked the smooth black skin of her arm. Then I reached up and took a strand of her wild hair in my hands. Her crazy hair was her signature statement and made her Allie, although sometimes she spent hours straightening it, which I couldn't figure out. Allie was Podium's star basketball player and was the tallest girl I'd ever known, with legs that, when we first started dating last spring, went up to my armpits. Seriously. No joke. I'd grown over the summer, but I was still two inches shorter than she was.

"I already told you, Allie-bean," I said, nuzzling my nose against her cheek. "We won."

We had started hanging out last spring when a mutual friend, Carrie, got into some trouble and had to leave school for a while. Allie and I had both missed her, so we'd talked at school, which led to hanging out on free weekends. I liked everything about Allie: her humour, her hair, the way she dressed in straight jeans and high-top runners, her passion for basketball, and the fact that she rarely drank, so I always had a designated driver. Kidding. But it *was* a bonus. All the guys thought so too.

She gave me a little slap on the shoulder. "I know that. I meant for *you*. Y'know, with colleges?"

"Ouch." I laughed. Then I took her hand in mine and leaned my head on the back of the sofa, letting my long hair fall behind me. If Allie was known for her crazy black hair, I was known for my unruly mop of blond hair. I glanced sideways at her, then took her hand in mine and ran my fingers over every one of her knuckles. "I briefly met with the coach from Syracuse," I finally said.

Allie immediately sat up straight. "What? You never told me that." She playfully punched my chest.

I laughed again and took both her hands in mine. Then I moved my head closer to her so our foreheads were touching and we were staring at each other. "It was brief," I whispered. "Nothing to tell."

Then I kissed her and my kiss was *not* brief. She tasted so amazing and smelled like soap: fresh clean soap. No perfume, just soap. While I kissed her, I gently pushed her back on the sofa until we were lying down beside each other. She wrapped her long legs around me, pulling my hips toward her. Then she put her hands under my T-shirt and ran them up and down my back, her nails lightly scratching my skin. We had yet to go the distance and I respected her for that, but I moaned anyway and ran my fingers through her hair. And I kissed her neck, her shoulder. She kissed me on the neck too and I hoped she would give me a hickey.

"Are you guys, like, making out?" a squeaky voice sounded from behind the sofa.

"Omigod, Grace, they *are* making out!"

Both Allie and I sprang to a sitting position and adjusted our clothing.

If I could have stood up and shoved my little sister, Marissa, toward the door, I would have. Instead I grabbed the throw blanket and covered my lower body with its immense hard-on. Then I yelled, "What do you want?"

Marissa stood there with her best girlfriend, Grace, and they had their hands over their mouths and were giggling. "You guys were making out. Na-than's making out." Marissa sang her words.

"Shut up," I said. "What are you doing down here, you little turd?"

"I'm gonna go up and tell Mom and Dad what you were doing." She put her hands on her hips. "And that you called me *turd*. Dad said you weren't supposed to call me that."

"It's not nice to be a tattletale, Marissa." Allie spoke softly.

Marissa's face fell and she looked as if she might cry. "I'm sorry, Allie."

Marissa loved Allie and followed her everywhere, asking her questions and talking to her, and Allie was always nice to her — too nice, if you asked me. I'd have told her to get lost and leave me alone ages ago if I were Allie.

"Come on, Grace," said Marissa. "Let's go upstairs. And leave the *lovebirds* alone." She was just about to leave when she said, "Dad *really* sent me down to tell you he wants to see you in his office." She put her hands on her hips and said, "Now!" in her best Dad impression.

Allie ran her hands down her thighs to smooth her jeans into place. "I've got to go anyway," she said, getting to her feet. "I've got early a.m. practice and still have tons of homework to do."

I was finally able to stand. "Yeah, me too," I mumbled. School was as painful as my father's wanting to see me.

As Marissa walked toward the stairs, Grace giggled and said, "Your brother is so-o-o skinny."

"My *brother* is like the skinniest guy ever. You should see his friends. They're *ginormous*. Nathan's got like protruding ribs."

"And really long hair like a girl's." They both started giggling, which was totally annoying.

When they were gone, Allie put her arm around me. "It's okay, Nathan," she whispered in my ear. "I've got a real thing for skinny guys with long hair." She tousled my hair, which was kind of embarrassing because she didn't have to reach up very far to do it.

"Skinny guys don't always have skinny parts," I said, puffing out my chest to make light of the situation when really, inside, I was crushed. By my little sister? How sad. I had stooped to an all-time low.

But then Allie said, "And don't I know that." She took my hand in hers. "Walk me to the door." Of course, this made me feel a whole lot better.

We hadn't even reached the front door when my dad barked at me from behind his office door. "Nathan!"

"Just wait," I yelled back. "Cranky or what?" I said to Allie. "He's got something stuck up his butt."

I didn't bother to kiss Allie at the door because I knew *someone* from my family would appear from nowhere like a bad wet fart. Most of the kids at Podium lived with billets, and I had thought I was one of the lucky ones to live at home. But tonight, I wished I lived with another family.

"Nathan!" My dad barked again.

"Coming," I snapped back. "Patience, patience," I muttered under my breath.

I entered his home office with a real crab on. Dad's demands really bugged me. I spoke first. "What do you want?"

The space was super-tidy as usual — my dad was so anal. There wasn't a paper out of place on his desk.

"Have a seat."

Uh-oh. This meant he wanted to have one of his chats. Hopefully it wasn't about sex.

As soon I was seated, he asked, "Have you thought about your application for the University of Calgary yet?" He paused. "Or have you thought about any other universities you might want to attend?"

"Dad, it's only September." I slouched in my seat. I had no intention of going to U of C or anywhere in Canada. I wanted a NCAA scholarship.

"Nathan, you need a plan B."

"No, I don't."

"I want you to do some research and pick three schools to apply to."

"Geez. I've got like six months. What is your problem? No one fills out their applications for university until after Christmas."

"November, Nathan. You want to get them in for early acceptance."

Just because he was anal didn't mean I had to be. He kept telling me that U of C was a good school and that's where he did his undergrad and that I should register for a bachelor of science so that I could be a doctor like him and take over the family practice. Med school was like seven years of schooling. No thanks. If I was going to university, it was to play lacrosse.

"I'm getting a scholarship, Dad."

He sat back in his chair and rolled a pencil with his long thin fingers. A skill he had perfected over his years of calling me into his office. I moved to leave. "You done?" I said, standing.

He put the pencil down. "Your mother had to clean out your bag and do your dirty laundry."

"Ho-ly. Why are you nitpicking me? I would have emptied it. I just got home yesterday."

He looked at me. "Point taken." His shoulders relaxed. "By the way, congratulations on the weekend," he said.

"Thanks." I relaxed a little too.

Sometimes my dad can be okay and we have moments where we actually get along, like when we go to the Queen Charlotte Islands on our annual summer fishing trip. Since I thought we might have a decent conversation now, I sat back down.

He smiled at me. "You must have been happy with the win."

"Yeah, it was great." I tossed my hair out of my eyes because I knew he liked it better when it wasn't hanging over my face. "We worked out some real kinks in our attack system. I got a few points in the last two games."

"Joe called today. He said Syracuse is looking at you as a possible."

My parents were probably the only people on the planet who called my coach Joe. Even Derkie's *wife* called him Derkie. I nodded. Why would he bring up U of C if he'd just talked to Derkie? Instead of arguing, which is what I really wanted to do, I said, "The scout talked to me after our last round robin game."

"Joe said you have a shot with them. Especially since you played well in the finals. What did the scout say to you?"

"He was interested."

"When will you get a more definite answer?"

"Soon," I said. No way would I tell him they weren't making a decision for another four to six months. "I'm pretty confident," I said.

He leaned forward and clasped his hands. "Unfortunately, Nathan, you take after me."

I slumped in the chair. I *hated* hearing that. Hated the reminder that I'd inherited his skinny body.

He obviously didn't notice that his words were irritating me because he just continued talking. "A scholarship would, of course, be terrific. You'll get a degree and then the years you've put into playing lacrosse will have been productive." He folded his hands together. "But that scholarship is not a given. You still need plan B."

I stood up again. Enough was enough. I turned my back on him and walked to the door. I had my hand on the doorknob when I heard his voice behind me.

"I'm proud of you, Nathan."

Shocked, I turned and immediately saw that he was serious.

"You're tough," he said. "Tougher than I ever was or ever could be. That toughness will take you far."

"Thanks," I mumbled.

Deep in thought about my skinny body, I made my way downstairs to my room in the basement, my man cave. It was just off our rec room and had a bathroom attached to it, which was awesome. I flopped down on my unmade bed and stared at the ceiling. Then I picked up the remote for my flat-screen television and turned on my favourite sports channel. One perk of living at home was having my own space and all the electronics. My room was a mess and I didn't even have to clean it up like so many of the guys who billeted. Plus a pile of clean laundry sat on my desk. I knew most of my friends had to do their own laundry.

As I flicked through station after station, I thought about my size. I might grow another inch and that was all the height I needed. What I needed now was bulk. And I needed it fast to get my scholarship. Like today, tomorrow, the next day.

I logged on to my computer and Googled "building muscle mass." Of course, there were numerous sites on weightlifting, but lifting didn't produce immediate results. No. I needed something else. My dad had said some things that made me want to take action, take control. Sure he wanted everything to be above board, but he just didn't understand. If I didn't act, didn't do something to help my body grow, I could be left behind. I wanted to be a professional lacrosse player and that was all I wanted. I had to get a scholarship to give me the four years to mature and fill out. I was not going to take no for an answer. I had been thinking about my options for a while now and knew what I needed to do.

Several hours later, I found Ryan's number and texted him.

"hey bro call me."

CHAPTER THREE

Although I hate school, as in going to classes and doing homework, I have to admit I like it for the social life, especially at Podium. It's a world full of athletes and friends who are as passionate about their sport as I am about mine. If I could only skip the academic part and take on just the sport and the social stuff, I would be happy. As it was, on Monday, I went in anxious to see my friends, my homework only half done.

I slid into the seat beside Carrie in English class. We'd been friends since the beginning of grade ten and I guess I considered her one of my best friends.

"Hey," she whispered. "How was your weekend?"

I gave a thumbs-up. "Awesome, Scary Carrie. Yours?"

She did this little tilty thing with her head, making her ponytail bounce. It was good to see the old Carrie back, boobs and all, although I didn't dare mention that to her because she had this thing about them being too big for her sport. I don't get it, but then guys don't. Not one guy in the school thought her boobs were too big or that she was the wrong shape for her sport. Just her psycho synchro friends thought that.

She leaned over and whispered, "I hung out with Aaron Saturday."

I raised my eyebrows. "Cool." I gave another thumbs-up. Aaron was a hockey player and a great dude. He'd come to Podium at the beginning of grade eleven and immediately hooked up with Carrie. They'd made a great couple until she had to leave. I knew she still liked him; she'd only told me a million times.

"I'll tell you about it after class."

I nodded and winked. Then I slouched in my seat, stretching my legs out in front of me, and pulled my sweatshirt hood over my head, letting my hair flop over my closed eyes. She cuffed me across the back of the head and said, "I suppose you're going to want my notes."

I nodded without opening my eyes. Carrie took great notes, so I didn't see why I had to stay awake and take them too. It seemed kind of redundant.

"You drive me crazy," she said. "You sleep and still get better grades than me."

I winked at her. "You do notes today and I'll find a way to pay you back." I closed my eyes again. School had always come easy for me — too easy, according to my dad. He was always harping at me to work harder and try for all 90s. I knew I didn't need *those* kinds of marks to get a scholarship. I needed to do well on the SAT tests.

Class finally ended and I stood and stretched. Laughing, Carrie shook her head at me. "Did you really sleep?"

"Yup." I yawned.

"How can you just *do* that?"

"I'm growing. I need sleep."

"I thought you looked a little bigger." She put her fingers around my biceps.

"That's the best thing I've heard all day." I flung my arm over her shoulder and we walked out of the classroom together. Carrie was short, so when I put my arm around her, it worked. She was the one girl who made me feel bigger than I really was. So many of the girls at Podium were big, like huge, because they were athletes. When we were in the hall, I knew I had to say *something* about her and Aaron. "So?" I asked. "Aaron?"

She grinned and did her happy shoulder bob. "We went to a movie." She had this habit of singing her words.

"What did you see?"

This time she frowned. "Doesn't matter what we saw."

"Oh man, please tell me you didn't make him sit through some awful chick flick."

She pulled away from me and slapped me on the arm. "No, I didn't make him sit through a *wonderful romantic comedy*. You guys could learn something from those movies y'know. We saw *Hangover 2*."

"That's good, Scary Carrie. You're learning."

"I was thinking" — she spoke with an excitement that I just couldn't do first thing in the morning — "that the four of us should do something this weekend."

"Sure," I replied. "I'm home."

"So is Aaron." She turned and started walking backwards so she was facing me. "You need to organize it with him, 'kay?"

"*Moi?*" I hated organizing movies and stuff. I'd rather let everything just happen.

Her eyes widened. "Yes, you. Now I gotta go. See you at lunch. And no notes if you don't figure out the weekend." With that, she took off down the hall at a speed I had no desire to keep up with.

Second block was math and I managed to get through it and stay awake, which was something to be proud of. Finally I entered the cafeteria and looked for Allie and Carrie and the rest of our group.

"Moore." I heard Ryan's voice behind me.

I turned. "Hey, what's shakin'?"

"Did you get my return text last night?" he asked.

"Yeah. Thanks," I replied.

"Did you manage to connect with the owner at Rocky's?"

I nodded.

He held up his fist and we bumped knuckles. "Between us."

"Gotcha."

I approached my table, the one my group always sat at, and plunked down my lunch. I sat beside Allie, making sure our legs were touching. Jax, Podium's crazy snowboarder, sat across from me, and Aaron Wong sat beside him at the end of the table. Some girl from the soccer team sat on the other side of Jax, so she was almost directly across from Allie. I'd seen her around the school, but I didn't know her name. She was new to our table. On Allie's other side was Carrie, and Hambone sat beside her at the very end of the table. There were some spots left at the table and usually Aaron's hockey buddy Kade Jensen showed up late.

"Heard you had a nap in English," said Allie, leaning

into me so our shoulders rubbed too.

"Sure did. And I feel a whole lot better for it." I opened up my lunch and pulled out my roast beef sandwich, piled high with cheese. No lettuce, no tomatoes, just dairy and protein. Another good thing about living at home, my mother always packed me a lunch I could stomach. Some of the guys got food that made them want to throw up because their billets just didn't know them well enough to know what they liked.

"I've got your notes," piped up Carrie. She leaned forward so I could see her give me this totally exaggerated wink.

I wanted her to hand them over, but that wasn't happening until I did my part of the bargain. I nodded, then lowered my head to eat.

"O-kay, what's shakin' between you two?" Allie, her eyes in narrow slits, looked from me to Carrie.

"Tell you later," whispered Carrie. Then she crunched a carrot.

"Hey, Parmita," said Allie, looking at the girl from the soccer team. Allie thumbed in my direction. "This is Nathan. He's a lacrosse player."

I did my usual cool one-finger salute.

Parmita gave me a little smile as she pulled a sack of vegetables out of her bag and what looked like a samosa that came from the frozen-food section of the grocery store. She shook her head at her lunch and said to Allie, "My billet mom thinks these will remind me of home. My mom has never made samosas in her life."

"Where you from?" I asked.

"Saskatoon," she said quietly.

"Her dad was born in India," said Allie, talking for Parmita. "And her mom is from Saskatoon."

Parmita lowered her head.

"Parmita's my new lab partner in chemistry," said Allie almost proudly. "And goalkeeper on the soccer team." Allie bit into a huge sub that spurted and dripped sauce all over the table.

"Gross," I said. "That landed on me."

"Did not." Allie laughed and wiped up the mess.

"I hope you're smart," I said to Parmita. "'Cause Allie will need help. She can't even eat a sub, let alone figure out a chemistry experiment. She might burn down the school."

"Hey!" said Allie. "I try my best." She scrunched up her sauce-soaked napkin and tossed it into the nearby garbage can, hitting it right in the middle. "Three points," she said.

"My turn," said Aaron. He jumped up and tossed his napkin but missed.

"Loser, Wong!" yelled Hambone. Then he stood on his chair and pretended to do a jumpshot.

Of course I had to be next and I balled up my lunch bag and threw it from behind my back. It landed on Parmita. I expected her to squeal or laugh or have some reaction, but she just picked it up and placed it on the table, which of course was even better because now it was a free game. I grabbed for it just as Hambone dove for it, and we ended up toppling over the table and spilling tons of crap on the floor. I was picking myself up when I saw a teacher coming toward us.

"Time to get to class," I said.

"Clean up the mess before you go," said Mr. Carruthers.

After tossing everything in the garbage, I walked out with Allie and Parmita, the most serious chick I'd ever met.

"Parm wants to be a doctor," said Allie. "She's like a total brainiac."

Doctor? I glanced at Parmita as she tucked her hair behind her ear, lowered her head, and stared at her feet. *Wow*, I thought. The girl was quiet and shy and nerdy, but she was a goalie, and goalies were a different breed. I wondered if my dad had been like that in high school too. Allie was going to stomp all over her but, hey, if she could grab herself a good mark out of the friendship, why not? The girl didn't talk much, but then, around Allie and Carrie, she probably couldn't get a word in anyway.

"You got practice after school?" Allie asked me, chewing on an oatmeal cookie. Allie ate nonstop all day and night.

"Nah," I said, tossing my head to get the hair out of my eyes. "Night off." When we hit the corner in the hall, where we were going in different directions, I said, "Catch ya later." Then I held up my hand to mimic phoning her.

"Later," Allie said, then headed off with Parmita.

Last class was a spare, so I left school early, got in my Jeep — another perk of living at home was having a good car to drive — and headed to Rocky's Supplement Store, the place Ryan had told me about. All the way there, I wondered what the guy was going to be like. Ryan had said he was cool.

What would I say to him?

The store was located in the northwest of Calgary, on 16th Avenue. Fortunately there was parking, so I pulled into a slot and shut off my car. Then I looked in the rearview mirror and tossed my head to put my hair into place.

"Okay, Nathan," I said out loud, "let's hope this is your lucky day."

Once inside the small, but well-stocked store, I walked around for a few minutes, staring at all the tubs of protein powder and jars of pills. It looked like every other supplement store I'd been in. I had Googled before coming and saw nothing that made it stand out. I guess my ticket was the guy working the desk, who at first glance was built like a wall of bricks, with a neck the same size as his head and a chest with rock-hard pecs. I walked slowly up to the counter.

"Can I help you?" His voice was deep and clipped.

"Is Terry Elliott around?" I was sure my voice came out really squeaky.

"You're talking to him, bro."

"My friend Ryan Duncan told me to come see you."

"Ah, Dunc. You're from his lacrosse team."

I nodded. At least Ryan had done the initial intros.

Terry sized me up and down, and instead of standing tall to look bigger, I shrunk into my shoes. This was unlike me, but I felt so out of my league. After his appraisal of me, Terry glanced around the store. No one was in it but us. His gaze came back to me and he raised one eyebrow. "What kind of help you looking for?" This time he spoke quietly.

I stood taller. I had done my homework and knew exactly what I needed. Now it was my turn to quickly glance around the store, even though I hadn't heard the front door open.

When I was positive we were alone, I turned back to Terry, leaned forward, and said softly, "Testosterone."

"You're awful young."

"Short term is all I want. Maybe just one cycle. I need to get big fast."

"You're sure." Terry narrowed his eyes.

"Positive."

"It can stop your growth."

"I doubt I'll grow much more than a couple inches," I said. "And I read where it usually takes more than one cycle to close the growth plates."

"Maybe not, kid."

What was with this guy? Why did Ryan send me here? Did *he* buy off this guy? I didn't get it. Terry was supposed to help, not shoot me down.

"I've done a ton of research," I said adamantly. "This is what I need."

The corner of Terry's mouth lifted in a little smirk. "Dunc said you were the scrappiest player he knew and you never backed down from anything. If I don't help you today, what are you going to do?"

"Find someone else who will. I know what I need."

"Okay. I wasn't put on this earth to be anyone's babysitter. I think your best bet is testosterone ethanate, one cycle for ten weeks. After the ten weeks, you'll need PCT — that's post-cycle therapy — to get your own testosterone going again. I take it you want injections?"

I shrugged. "What do you recommend?"

"Injections are more effective and don't cause as much liver damage, but not everyone is a fan of needles."

"I'm okay with them."

"Come by my home tonight — 122 Greenborough Drive — after six. And bring cash."

"How much?"

"Seven hundred and twenty dollars."

The amount made me gulp. "Will I need —" The doorbell chimed, and my question was killed.

"So let me show you some powders I think would be good for you," said Terry.

I followed him to the shelf with all the protein powders. The man who had entered the store looked our way. Under my breath, I kept muttering the address. He had only told it to me once.

"Be with you in a second," said Terry, smiling at the new customer.

"No problem," said the man.

Terry picked out a protein powder that claimed to develop muscle mass and handed it to me. "You *will* need this," he said. "It's important for the growth."

I paid and left quickly, saying the address over and over all the way to my Jeep. As soon as I got in, I yanked out my phone. The bravado I'd had in the store suddenly turned to nerves. My hands shook and I could hardly punch the address into my phone. Was I really going through with this? I'd have to dip into my college savings account to pay for the juice.

My heart pounded through my T-shirt. One cycle was all I would need to get me through the fall field season, perfect for attracting the attention of Syracuse. Once I had my scholarship secured, I would stop the stuff and just work out extra hard in the gym.

Was I rationalizing? I could hear my father's voice in my head. *"Stop rationalizing. Honesty is the only way to live your life."*

"Sorry, Dad." I pounded my steering wheel with my fist. "I have to do this."

CHAPTER FOUR

At exactly 6:00 p.m., I pulled up in front of a small box-like white and brown house. Two cars sat in the driveway: a silver Toyota Corolla and a black Lexus van. I figured Terry drove the Lexus van. Did he make that much money selling this stuff illegally? I knew he'd marked mine up because I'd read the cost online. I didn't care.

I knocked on the door and tapped my foot as I waited. All afternoon I'd convinced myself that I was doing the right thing. Short-term, I had told myself over and over.

Terry answered the door and ushered me into a small hallway. He didn't direct me any further inside, so I remained where I was.

He handed me a bag. "Instructions for injections are inside. I provided you with enough needles as well. It's oil-based so it might hurt when you inject."

"Okay," I said, then handed him the wad of cash from my pocket.

Terry quickly counted it, then said, "Hit the gym while on it to help the muscles grow. Eat protein and drink lots of protein shakes. You might get sore at the injection site, so when you want to inject is up to you. Morning, night, the choice is yours."

"Okay."

"Injections are intramuscular. Glutes are the best. I do it on my own with a mirror, but I suggest you get some help. When you inject, before you plunge, pull it back just a bit and check for blood. If there is any, pull the needle out without injecting. It means you've nicked a vein, and if you inject, the juice will go straight to your heart, which can be deadly."

I nodded because I couldn't speak. It was as if someone had drilled a lacrosse ball at me and I had caught it in my throat. I felt like an idiot.

Finally he smiled a tiny smirk. "So you go to Podium. What're your goals?"

"Scholarship. Then pro."

"Pro is for the big boys. You definitely need some meat on your bones, kid. And muscles do protect. Lots of pro athletes take this."

"How long before I see any results?" I asked.

"Could be as early as a couple of weeks. Any random dope tests in the near future?"

I shook my head. "Podium doesn't do them," I said. My only goal was to secure the scholarship. My school visit would probably be in the spring and by then I'd be clean. But even then, most colleges didn't have the money to be doing random dope tests.

"That's a good thing." He ushered me to the door. "If you need help, don't call me."

"What about side effects?" I asked.

"Some guys get them all, some guys get a few. Everyone is different and you won't know your reaction until you inject. You might get acne and you might get irritable. Who knows? The most easygoing guy can be the one to snap." He slapped my back and opened the door for me. "It's a crapshoot, bro." Before I could say goodbye, the door was shut.

Driving home, I felt as if my brain was going to burst out of my head. What was I doing? Or should I say, what was I *going* to do?

When I got home, I gave a few brief hellos and went right to my man cave. I closed my door tightly, then logged on to my computer. Allie had texted me earlier but I didn't reply to her. Being a purist, she would not agree. Well, she didn't have to know. This was *my* deal, *my* life. She just so happened to be one of the lucky ones who had the exact right body for her sport.

As I read everything I'd already read at least ten times, my stomach tightened. I knew a little bit about the side effects, but I wondered how I would handle them. Perhaps if I had a plan, I could deal with them. Terry did say not all the side effects happened to everyone. Acne I could blame on hormones. Little prepubescent girl breasts known as bitch tits I could hide under T-shirts. Sexual aggression could be blamed on being a teenage boy. And a foul mood could be blamed on being a teenager too, right? I scrolled through the article and read that some of the irritability was just short bursts. Perhaps I could control these by walking away, clenching my fists, or even counting. Shrunken testicles? Yikes. Maybe I'd be one of the lucky ones who didn't get *that* side effect. I sat back and wrung my hands together.

If I didn't inject, I would've just wasted $720.

I have to get bigger. I have to do this to get a scholarship.

I opened the bag Terry had given me. For the next fifteen minutes, I read the instructions over and over until my eyes were crossed and my head ached. The injection had to be intramuscular. Quads? Glutes? Which one should I do? Glutes were a bigger muscle. Quads were easier because I could see them. I was supposed to inject twice a week and I could do morning or evening. When would be best for me? Another big decision. It could hurt. So if I had practice, then it wouldn't be good in the morning? I didn't want to be sore for practice or workout; Blackie might become suspicious. I could probably fool Derkie longer because of equipment and baggy clothes.

Okay, really think about this. Be practical.

Suddenly I heard my dad from upstairs, yelling at me about something. "Just a second," I bellowed back.

Then I heard him coming down the stairs. The guy was the most impatient creature on the globe! I quickly shoved the bag under my comforter and lay on my bed with my hands clasped behind my head.

"What's up Daddio?" I tried to sound casual even though my heart was thwacking under my T-shirt.

He stood at my door. "I need you to work in the office this weekend. What's your schedule like?"

For a little cash, I often worked in the office where he saw patients, filing and stuff like that. It was a superboring job but I liked the money. I did a little of my usual moaning and groaning before I said, "Sure, okay." I forced out a sigh. "I'm off the hook for games. I think we might have a practice but that's it."

Dad raised his eyebrows at me, obviously shocked that I was saying yes so quickly. Usually I moaned a lot longer.

"Having a girlfriend," I said, "means I need a few loonies."

"Gotcha." He did a thumbs-up, trying to be cool. It was so lame when he did stuff like that. "You need money to pay for dates. Well, good, Nathan. You have to treat women right, son, and take them out and pay the tab. And your help at my office works for me."

He was almost out my door before he said, "Oh yeah, Mom said dinner would be ready in five minutes." He looked at his watch. "It's already seven. Where's the time go?"

"No kidding," I said. "I'm starving. What's Mom making?"

"Some sort of pasta. A new recipe."

As soon as my father left, I sat up and put my head in my hands. He couldn't find out, he just couldn't.

After dinner, Marissa cleared the table and I was to help my mother load the dishwasher. My mom was this calm no-nonsense mom who loved supporting causes, like the SPCA and women's shelters. She also supported my lacrosse and often stuck up for me when my dad started railing on me about going to university. She would tell him to give me time to pursue my passion. I loved her and respected everything about her.

"How are you and Allie doing?" she asked, rinsing a plate.

I took the plate from her and stacked it in the dish-washer. "Good," I answered.

She looked at me and smiled. "She's a nice girl. I really like her."

I grinned. "I kinda like Allie-bean too."

"Treat her right, now. It's important to be good to women. Open doors and give her compliments. And don't forget —"

"Mo-om, I know all this stuff, okay? I do all those things 'cause" — I playfully slapped her on the shoulder — "you taught me well."

She laughed. "I'm just reminding you so it becomes . . . What's the term you use in sports?" She pointed her finger at me and smiled. "Oh yeah, muscle memory."

After the dishes were in the washer, I headed back down to my man cave. Again, I shut my door as tight as I could. Time ticked by slowly. I tried to do homework but there was no way I could concentrate. Finally, at exactly 10:00 p.m., I pulled out the syringe and liquid testosterone. My hands shook when I measured out the recommended dosage and filled the syringe. Then I set it on my desk and stared at it. Was I really going to do this? My stomach did crazy somersaults. What possessed me to think that this was a good thing? I actually hated needles. And I had to give it to myself.

I wished I could call my dad down to help.

Do it and get it over with, Nathan. No pain, no gain.

It's a low dosage. Everything will be fine. You're just helping your system for a few months.

I stood up and positioned myself so my back was to the

mirror. In the bag Terry had given me was a photo showing how to self-inject. The trick was to draw a square to mark the spot. I pulled my boxers down a bit and drew a square with a black marker. For a second I stared at it, then I grabbed the flesh of my butt. I picked up the needle with my other hand, pressed it to the middle of the square, and jabbed it in. I inhaled. Before plunging the testosterone into my body, I drew the syringe back a little like Terry had told me, and exhaled when I saw there was no blood.

"Come on, Nathan," I whispered to myself. "Get it over with."

I closed my eyes, sucked in a breath, and pressed the syringe. Hard. Did it go in? Had I done it? Was all of it in me? Suddenly I heard footsteps upstairs. My heart pounded. My blood raced. My body trembled.

Hands shaking, I quickly pulled out the needle, ignoring the stinging sensation, and glanced around for somewhere to put it.

Then I realized no one was coming downstairs. The footsteps upstairs had stopped. My breathing started to slow. I wiped my brow. This was crazy. I was a nervous wreck. I sat down on the bed, fully expecting to feel pain, but all I felt were some twinges.

I'd done it. I'd injected my first dose. There was no turning back now.

When my breathing was back to normal, I glanced around my room. I needed a secure place to store everything. In the back of my closet was a little end table where I stored stuff, mainly just crap. I could shove the juice things to the back of that drawer and no one would find them. I glanced around my room. What if I put the stuff in something to make it look like something else?

In the corner of my room, on the floor, shoved into the corner, was a plastic bag from a video game store. I had just bought a new game the other day. *Perfect*, I thought. I carefully put the bottle and extra syringes in the bag. The old syringe would have to be thrown out tomorrow in the bottom of some random garbage can. I stuffed it in another bag and jammed it into my backpack.

Now I had to go to sleep.

I lay on my bed and stared at the ceiling. I'm not sure what I was expecting, but something. Jitters. Weird vibrations in my body. Something, anything, to tell me that I had just injected a hormone into my body.

But honestly, I felt nothing. Or at least it felt like I felt nothing, if that makes any sense. It took over an hour, but finally I fell into a fitful sleep.

CHAPTER FIVE

The first thing I did when I woke up the next morning was touch my butt. It wasn't too sore, so that was a good thing. In the shower I scrubbed off the black marker I had used to mark the injection spot.

School was boring as usual, but I kept my mind busy thinking about what was going to happen to me in a few weeks. At lunch I hooked up with the usual gang, and that soccer girl Parmita, who seemed to be quickly becoming Allie's new best friend. Allie and Carrie had been super-close, like inseparable, before Carrie had left. When she returned, they couldn't quite get their friendship back on track. Not that it was any of my business.

"So?" whispered Carrie when I sat down.

"So . . . what?" I pulled out my sandwich and the extra protein bars I'd thrown in my bag. *Does she know something?* My blood started to race through my body at a speed only a Porsche can reach.

She jerked her head to the side and I looked down the table, spotting Aaron at the other end. Immediately I calmed down. Right. Aaron. I had totally forgotten our deal. I nodded. "Gotcha," I said.

"You forgot." She punched me.

"Ouch." I faked like it hurt.

She opened her eyes wide. "You need to talk to him soon," she whispered. "Like today."

I gave her a thumbs-up.

Now Allie leaned into me and whispered, "It's all she's talked about all morning."

Carrie narrowed her eyes at Allie and me. "Are you guys talking about me?"

"Nope," said Allie. Then she turned to Parmita. "Hey, Parm, you want to meet in the chemistry lab last block?"

Parmita nodded. "Absolutely," she said. Usually she spoke in a monotone, but when she talked to Allie, her voice had expression. I wondered how anyone could be so serious all the time and what Allie had to talk to her about. Chemistry wasn't something you could actually discuss for hours at length, or even minutes, at least not in my books.

The rest of the lunch hour progressed as it always did. Hambone threw food. Jax counted to ten while burping. Scary Carrie squealed. Wong tossed everyone's lunch kit in the garbage and pretended he was an NBA star on a video game. Allie talked non-stop and ate everyone's leftovers. And the new girl, Parm, as Allie had nicknamed her, didn't speak.

All through lunch, I had these really weird moments where I glanced at my friends and knew I had a secret. In a way, it made me sad. But it would have to stay that way. No exceptions. The only one who knew anything was Ryan, but he didn't count because he wanted it kept a secret as much as I did. I wondered if he got a commission from Terry.

Lunch ended and when Aaron bodychecked me on the way out, we hit a table and knocked it over. We laughed, saw the teacher coming, and righted it. Then he took off before I could say anything to him about Saturday night. As I sauntered to my last class of the day, I pulled out my phone to text him, but it was dead. What a drag. I hated having a dead phone. I made a mental note to text him later. *Yes, later,* I thought. There were certain things, like homework and setting up dates, that could always be done later.

After school I went right to the dressing room and quickly changed. I swear I was out of my clothes and in my lacrosse gear in less than a minute because I was worried about that stupid square on my butt showing. Once dressed, I headed out to the field with my stick and ball. As I jogged, I cradled my stick and worked on my lateral foot moves. The sun shone, heating my skin, and the fall air was a perfect temperature. Although I loved these amazingly sunny days, I admit I was one of the crazy players who loved playing in the rain. Rain made the ground slick and so easy to slide on.

As soon as Derkie saw me, he motioned for me to come over. Immediately I ran over to him, stopping right in front of him. I pushed my mouth guard out of my mouth. "What's up, Derkie?"

"I want you to lead warm-up."

"Sure. Anything specific?"

"Lots of running and ball handling. We're working on offence today."

I nodded. "Got it." I ran back to my teammates, who were now passing back and forth to one another and shooting on the goalie. I called in my assistant captains, letting them in on the plan. I always made eye contact when I was talking to them, but today, when I looked at Ryan, I barely glanced at him before I looked away.

I continued talking, telling them that we were going to run lines before breaking into groups to do some passing drills. "Derkie wants everything crisp and snappy," I said.

For some reason, I felt totally jacked for the practice, so I ran a tougher warm-up than usual. We ran lines, performed passing drills, then worked on dodge moves. The guys were really sweating by the time it was over and I could tell Derkie was happy with me. Dodge drills were my best because I had quick feet.

After fifteen minutes he called us in. "I want to start with three attackers and two defence. Moore, Hamilton, Spooner, you line up first against Duncan and Walker."

Walker was the biggest guy on our team. Six-four and weighing in at 240, in all honesty, he looked like a gorilla. He was slow too, and I could always beat him with a simple V-cut or roll. He turned like a cruise ship changing direction.

We jogged to our places and let Andre Beaulieu, our goalkeeper, get set up. Once he lowered his mask, I cradled the ball, then immediately passed to Hambone. He caught it and fired off a pass to Jimmy Spooner on our far side. We continued the quick hard passes as we moved forward, trying to get through the defence. I saw Normie Walker coming toward me, stick in the air, ready to pounce on me, slash my stick, and make me drop the ball. In a slick manoeuvre, I darted to my left, cut to the right, and when I did my roll dodge, I switched my hands on my stick to protect the ball and create an opportunity to make the perfect pass. As soon as I had completed my roll, I sent a feed pass off to Hambone so he could take a quick stick shot on goal. He fired it just as I felt Walker's hit.

I heard Derkie yell, "You got to stay on him, Walker. Take him out of the play. He's a twig and you're a log. Don't let him get close for the rebound."

I bounced off Walker's stick. *Just you wait, Derkie. I won't be a twig for long.* I scooted by Walker and ran to the net.

Hambone had already passed it to Spooner on the far side and he was winding up for a shot. I strode forward for the rebound, feeling the shove from behind. I stumbled for a nanosecond, then righted myself and kept moving. Andre made the save, not allowing a rebound, and Derkie blew the whistle. Our turn was over. We ran off to the side to get back in line. I breathed deeply so I could be prepared to fight again. As I waited for our next turn, I jogged on the spot.

Am I getting stronger already?

The rest of the practice went well, and in the change room afterwards, Hambone gave me a high-five.

"You were hard on your stick today," he said.

"Thanks." Then for some reason, I blurted out, "Must be the protein powder drink I bought." Why I said that, I don't know. Then to make matters worse, I didn't shut up. "I think I'm finally getting used to my height too." I felt like I was having a bad case of verbal diarrhea.

"Which protein did you buy?" Hambone asked, oblivious.

Why did I say anything? What's wrong with me? Just shut up, Nathan. Shut up.

"Muscle power." I flexed. "These babies will soon be huge."

Hambone laughed. "Okay. I'll believe that when I see it."

I snapped my towel at him before heading to the shower. As the water streamed over my head, running down my face, I smiled to myself. I had done it; I had created a reason for the strength I was soon going to have.

On Thursday I pulled out my stashed bag, filled the syringe, and gave myself another injection — and it seemed easier. Much easier. Two down, eighteen to go. How many, I wondered, until something happened physically, until I could see a change? Right then, I thought I *felt* a change, but I wasn't sure if I was just imagining things. To know it was working, I guess I needed tangible evidence, like bulging biceps and huge quads.

I put everything away in its hiding spot. Once again I put the used needle in my backpack to throw in a garbage can on the way to school. Then I flopped down on my bed.

My phone buzzed so I picked it up. Text from Carrie.

"we on for sat?"

"yup"

"took ya long enough"

"yeah but done deal. now time to buck up with english"

But before seeing any movie on Saturday, I had to work in my dad's office.

I arrived at his office at 9:00 a.m. My father was good at cruel punishment. It was my one Saturday off from practice and he had given me explicit instructions to be there at nine. He had gone in earlier because he liked to run before work, so I drove over myself. When I arrived, I was still half asleep.

At exactly one minute after nine, I started my tedious job of filing. Paper after paper I stuck into files. Talk about boring. The minutes went by so slowly it was painful. By noon I was starving.

Dad popped his head into the small office where I was working. "You hungry?" he asked.

"Oh yeah," I said.

"You want me to get pizza?"

I looked up from my stack of paper. "Sure."

Once my dad was gone, I leaned back in my chair, balancing on the back two legs. I wasn't touching another paper until I ate. I slammed my chair down and rested my head on the desk to have a nap. My dad appeared twenty minutes later, smiling and holding a steaming pizza box. I looked up.

"Got your favourite." His eyebrows shot up. "Meat lovers supreme."

"Awesome," I replied. Something pinched me inside. If he knew what I had injected this week and how I had drained my bank account of so much money, he wouldn't be so nice.

We hunkered down and I ate the first piece without saying a word.

Halfway through my second piece, he said, "How's school going?"

I wiped my mouth with a napkin. "Fine," I said.

"How are your marks?"

I shrugged. "It's early. I haven't handed in much."

"Grade twelve is an important year. You'll have to write your government diploma exams."

"I know. I'll be fine. How was your run this morning?"

"Good. Ten miles."

"Wow. You entered in any more races?"

"I'm trying to qualify for the Boston Marathon."

We continued eating pizza and chatting, and I was extremely grateful he didn't talk to me about Allie and condoms.

I ate six pieces of pizza and my dad ate two.

"You must be growing," he said to me.

Perfect. If I could convince everyone I was having a growth spurt, no one would notice a thing. "Yeah, for sure," I said. Then I patted my chest to be funny. "Huge. I will be huge soon." I tried to sound like a caveman.

He laughed, shook his head at me, and pointed to the files. "Back to work, Hulk."

The afternoon went faster than the morning and soon my stack of papers was filed. I stood, stretched, and yawned, then yanked on my jacket. "Gotta fly," I said.

"Thanks again, Nathan." He patted me on the back. "I really appreciate the help."

"No problemo." I tossed my hair out of my eyes. Then I held up my fist, knuckles forward. "Cheque in the mail?"

He bumped my knuckles with his and gave me his quirky, but nerdy smile. "I think the money got spent on that new lacrosse stick."

I groaned. Then he winked, pulled out his wallet, and gave me two twenties. "Get out of here. Take Allie out."

"Thanks, Dad." And before he could talk to me about anything else, I headed for the door.

"Ciao for now!" I yelled as I bolted outside.

When I got in my car, I leaned my head back. Why did he have to be so nice *now*?

I picked up Allie at her billets' house just before seven, over thirty minutes late. I'd had a nap when I got home and forgot to set my alarm. We were supposed to be meeting Aaron and Carrie at the movie theatre.

"Why are you late?" she asked as she buckled up her seat belt. "Did you get stuck in traffic or something?"

The accusatory tone of her voice, for some weird reason, grated me and I bristled. "Yeah," I snapped back. "Glenmore was brutal."

She frowned. "Chill out. I just asked why you were late. You don't have to bite my head off."

I'd never talked to Allie like that before. As fast as the irritability arrived, it left.

"Sorry," I said. "I had to work for my dad all day."

She glanced at me. "It's okay. Carrie's just freaking that we're not coming."

Allie's phone buzzed. She looked at the caller ID on the screen, then pressed the green button. "We'll be there in ten," she said.

"The movie doesn't start until seven-thirty," I said. "Tell her to relax."

"I know," said Allie, rolling her eyes. "But you know

Carrie. I think she's trying way too hard with Aaron and it's all going to backfire."

"That's Aaron's problem," I said. "He'd be stupid not to go back with her."

"Yeah, but that's coming from Carrie's biggest fan."

Allie's sarcastic tone made me glance at her, and again I felt a rush of anger pulse through me. She was slouched in the seat, looking straight ahead. I focused on the road and gripped the steering wheel hard. *Don't speak, Nathan, don't speak.*

But I couldn't stop myself. "What's *that* supposed to mean?"

She glanced at me and I saw the shocked look in her eyes. I wished I could take the words back. I inhaled. I was snapping at her for no good reason.

"Nothing," she said. "Sorry I said it."

"Sometimes you say things that make no sense." I spoke in a gentler tone, trying to soften the last comment.

"I said I was sorry."

By the time we arrived at the movie theatre and were out of the Jeep, I had totally calmed down. I took Allie's hand and that seemed to warm us up a bit. When we walked into the theatre, Carrie was waiting at the bottom of the escalator for us and there was no Aaron in sight.

"He's not here yet," she moaned.

I put my arm around her. "He's coming. He just sent me a text. He got held up at hockey practice."

Carrie put her hand to her chest. Her nicely rounded chest, which was bulging out of her low-cut T-shirt, I might add. Just the sight of her big boobs made my mouth go dry.

"Oh good," she said. "I'm so nervous."

"Don't be nervous." I put my arm around her. "Just be your sweet self."

"Oh my gawd." Allie rolled her eyes. "That's pathetic. Just be sweet?" She looped her arm through Carrie's. "Come on, girl, let's get popcorn."

We headed up the escalator and I said I would get in line for the tickets if they got the popcorn. The entire time I was in line, I thought about how harsh I'd been with Allie and how it was so out of character. I would have to learn to control whatever was going on inside me. Deep in thought, I was only jolted back to reality when I felt a little bump from behind.

I turned. "Hey dude," I said to Aaron.

"What's up?" he asked.

"Not much."

"What movie we seeing?"

"Action all the way."

"Good man." He patted my shoulder.

"Allie and Carrie are getting the popcorn."

"I need food too," said Aaron. "Real food."

I held up one thumb. "Hot dog with onions."

The movie was great. Allie and I snuggled and she put her head on my shoulder. I wished we were alone in the theatre. Once I started thinking about being alone with her, I had to touch her. I ran my hand up and down her thigh and she giggled until Carrie leaned over and told us to shut up.

After the movie we walked hand in hand behind Carrie

and Aaron, who were walking ahead of us at least three feet apart *and* looking quite stiff with each other. Some fences couldn't be mended. Her eating issues and lies about it had done something to them as a couple, and it didn't look as if the relationship was reparable. I felt for Carrie. She was an athlete who would do anything for her sport and had stuck with Aaron when he had his team issues. But really, none of it was my concern.

"I don't think it's going so well for them," whispered Allie.

"Yeah. They should probably call it quits."

"They were an awesome couple. She's being too pushy. If she would just stop pestering the guy, he might come around."

"That's Carrie," I said. "She's over the top in everything she does. Cutting him slack just ain't her style. Maybe he's the one who should cut *her* a little."

"You always stick up for her!"

Out of the corner of my eye, I glanced at Allie. What was wrong with her? Every time I said anything about Carrie, she got mad. I let go of her hand and shoved my hands into my pockets. "Isn't that what being a friend is?"

"Whatever." Allie rolled her eyes.

We continued walking, not holding hands. Ahead of us, Carrie was walking with her arms across her chest and Aaron had his head turned away from her. Suddenly Carrie stopped and yelled, "So that's it, then?"

Aaron finally looked at her. "Guess so," he said loud enough for us to hear.

"Uh-oh," said Allie.

"Sparks are flying," I said.

Stopping in the middle of the parking lot, Carrie turned to face us. By now we were beside the fighting couple. "Aaron doesn't want to come for pizza!" she snapped.

"I didn't say that," retorted Aaron.

"Yes, you did!"

Aaron shook his head, obviously exasperated. "No, I didn't."

Allie stepped forward, holding up her hands. "Hold on, you two. Let's all go and try to resolve this."

Always to the rescue, that was my Allie-bean. I rocked back on my heels. I wasn't big on resolving things that had a shelf life, and if you asked me, Carrie and Aaron had expired. Allie was the only one still clinging to the reunion and I couldn't figure out why she cared.

"I'm just going home," mumbled Aaron.

I gave him a thumbs-up. "Gotcha," I said.

Carrie tossed her hair and stuck her nose in the air. "I'd lo-o-ove to go for pizza," she said with more attitude than necessary.

"Meet ya there." I flipped my keys in the air and caught them behind my back.

When we got in my Jeep, Allie glared at me. "Why did you just let Aaron off the hook?"

"He didn't want to go." I started the engine.

"You should've talked him into it."

I backed out of the parking spot. "Not my deal."

"You would've convinced Carrie though," she said.

My insides surged. Why was she always harping about Carrie? "What is wrong with you!?" I yelled, my voice pinging off the car windows.

Allie slid down in her seat, hunching her shoulders to her ears. "You don't have to scream at me." Her voice was a mere whisper. She glanced at me out of the corner of her eye. "Nathan, I've never seen this side of you before. I don't like it."

I gripped the steering wheel. "Just shut up about Carrie!"

"Nathan, stop being so mean."

Allie looked as if she might cry. She fiddled with the ties on her jacket.

I ran my hand through my hair and breathed deeply. I swear I could feel my blood slowing down inside my body. "Just leave their relationship alone, okay?" I said in a much quieter voice. "It's none of our business."

"I was just trying to hook them up again because they belong together."

"I get that, and I'm sorry I yelled," I said, sighing. I reached for her hand. "I just wish I knew what I was doing next year. I think it's stressing me out."

"But you never get stressed out," she said. "You're the most easygoing guy around. Don't worry, you'll get a scholarship." Allie let me hold her hand for a second before she pulled it away to let me drive. She was big on safe driving, which meant two hands on the steering wheel.

"I guess everyone's acting weird tonight," she said. "Me included."

"It's the full moon." I started howling.

She playfully punched my arm. "Stop that."

The Jeep was on an easy straight stretch of road now, so I put my arm around her. "So, bottomless pit, you want pizza?"

She leaned over and kissed my cheek. Again she took my hand and put it back on the wheel. "Get me there safely and I bet I can eat more than you."

CHAPTER SIX

By my third week and sixth injection, my body decided to break out in a massive amount of zits. I noticed the "backne" on a Friday when I was getting ready for school and caught a glimpse of my back in the mirror. I'd seen a few zits on my back earlier in the week but nothing like this.

"Holy crap!" I said to myself. "That is so gross." My inflamed back was red, blotchy, and disgusting.

For the past week I had injected in my thigh because my butt was getting sore, and so I hadn't been staring at my back in the mirror. Almost a quarter of the way through the cycle, I had seen some gains in my muscle size and was telling everyone it had to do with the new protein powder. But this? How was I going to explain the hot-and-ready pepperoni pizza on my back?

I groaned and threw on my shirt. At least I'd seen the zits and could try to hide that area of my body somehow. I had to think of something. Lies. Lies. Lies. They made my stomach heave.

As I turned around to face the mirror, I leaned in. Zits

marked my face too, but not like the ones on my back. My mother had noticed and immediately gone to the drugstore for products. She was the best. Honestly. A punch, like a hard cross-check, hit my gut. My dad couldn't find out about the testosterone because he would freak and throw a medical textbook at me, but my mom, she couldn't find out because she would be disappointed in me.

Carrie was already in her seat when I slipped into English class. I slid into the desk behind her and she immediately turned around. "Hey," she said, "I'm going to your game tonight."

I nodded and gave her my one-finger wave.

"I think Jax is coming too," she said. "Maybe we can do something after."

Sometimes we went out as a team but not always, especially on a Friday night. More often than not, on the weekend, a bunch of us went out, including teammates and other Podium athletes. "Sure," I said. "Let's see what shakes."

Since the movie night, Aaron and Carrie were kaput. Now she seemed to be hanging out with Jax. I liked Jax. He was this cool snowboarding guy who was on a bunch of crazy snowboarding videos, riding rails and doing flips. I'd watched one of his competitions last year at WinSport Arena and thought the jumps and moves he did were pretty awesome. I also thought he and Carrie might make a good couple.

"When did Allie leave for Edmonton?" Carrie asked, which I thought was kind of weird since usually she knew everything about Allie. But then again, I did have the inside scoop that Allie hadn't been talking to Carrie much since Carrie and Aaron's split, and girls could hold grudges for reasons that weren't really reasons.

"This morning," I replied. "Big game there tonight."

"She never talks to me anymore." Carrie doodled on her notebook. Then she turned to look at me again. "Can you talk to her for me?"

"Um ..." There was no way I wanted to get in the middle of a cat fight. But I liked Carrie and could see she was really bugged. "And what exactly am I supposed to say?"

Carrie shrugged. "I don't know. Just tell her I miss her."

"I guess that would be easy enough to do."

She tilted her head and smiled at me. "You're the best." She paused, but as usual, not for long. "Hey, have you finished the questions on the first four chapters of *Moby Dick*?"

I tapped my pen on the desk. "Um, I planned on doing them this weekend. I haven't even started reading the book. Have you?" For the past three weeks, concentrating had become an issue. I'd get down to my man cave and spend hours on the computer looking up everything and anything to do with testosterone. I knew my grades were slipping but figured I had time to get them back on track. I'd always been able to pull them up with just a little work.

"Yeah," she said. "It's okay. I prefer current books over the classics."

"Me too," I said. Then I grinned. "Or graphic novels."

"Ha ha. We should lobby to be able to choose between a graphic novel and Shakespeare."

"Now that would definitely help my mark," I said.

"Your English marks were great last year."

"Yeah."

The sound of the teacher's voice halted our conversation.

I was so keyed up to play that I arrived at the field early for the evening game and found myself alone in the change room. I breathed a sigh of relief. I whipped off my shirt and quickly put on my dry-fit undershirt. Once my back was covered, I leaned back, pressed my head against the concrete wall, and closed my eyes. All was good.

Now I needed to focus on the game. We were playing a real physical team, the Vipers from Hamilton, Ontario, and they were known for hard hits that weren't always clean. I looked down at my quads as I flexed my leg. And just like that, the muscle seemed to pop at me. I blinked. Holy crap. I had quads! I had been waiting and wondering when I would really notice. Sure, my weight was up eighteen pounds, but I was waiting for that muscle to show. I flexed my biceps and immediately noticed they had grown as well.

Yes! I was filling out.

To date, everyone totally believed my story about sucking back the protein powder shakes and the heavy lifting. And in all honesty, I *was* sucking back the shakes, and I *was* working out in the gym.

I stuck in my earbuds, leaned back against the wall again, closed my eyes, and listened to the Black Eyed Peas song "I've Got a Feeling." It was my favourite pump-up song.

Partway through the tune, my teammates began entering the change room. I could tell they were stoked too. I pulled out my earbuds and stood up. "We're gonna rock tonight!"

Hambone gave me a high-five and immediately started to get into his lacrosse gear.

When we hit the field, the lights shining brightly, the night air cool and refreshing, we were in full stride. The crowd cheered. We averaged anywhere from three hundred to five hundred fans, which wasn't bad for high school field lacrosse. Hockey was the number-one draw at Podium, but then hockey was a bigger sport in Canada. Didn't matter much to me though, because I loved running, catching, throwing, and drilling a hard rubber ball at an opening in the net. I was proud of my sport and knew we battled the popularity odds every day. But the fact was, lacrosse was a huge draw at Syracuse University, and the head scout was in the stands again tonight. Derkie had told me he was looking at me and a kid from Hamilton.

One day I was going to play in front of huge crowds.

I led my team through a warm-up, then took my place on the field as part of the starting lineup. I jiggled my legs as we listened to some local girl sing "O Canada." Then it was time to rumble.

As centre I crouched down at midfield, holding my stick flat on the ground with the back of my stick pocket pressed up against the opposing centre's stick. I had watched enough videos on the guy to know he was quick but totally beatable. For days I'd known my strategy for the faceoff, and I was going to clamp the ball to gain control of it. As soon as it was placed between the sticks, I geared up for the signal. I had to be quick. Like real quick. The ref signalled the game to begin and I pushed the back of my stick on the ball. I had him. I'd beaten him by a split second. And that was all the time I needed. Hambone ran forward and I winged a pass to him. He caught it with ease and passed off ASAP to Spooner, who was already in full stride. I pushed through my opposing centre and within three strides was running full tilt. We wove our way down the field, sending clean and crisp passes to one another. No one held on to the ball for long. We didn't want a turnover.

Closer to the net, I saw the defence and they were huge. Massive. But I was ready. When I saw Hambone moving forward with the ball, looking for someone to pass to, I did a quick V-cut to get by my defence. I almost made a totally clean cut, but then I felt the cross-check on my shoulder. I smacked the guy's stick and was surprised when I knocked it down enough to be able to push by and out of his reach. They were playing a man-to-man system and I had him beat. Now I was wide open.

Hambone saw me and nailed a feed pass to me. In one swift motion, I shot it toward the goal. The goalie stuck out his arm and blocked the shot, letting out a rebound — but no one was at the front of the net. Where was Spooner?

Then I saw him out of the corner of my eye. He was moving in too late.

The ball was picked up by a player from the Vipers, but Hambone knocked him hard. I saw the loose ball, scooped it up, and fired it at the net, but again the goalie made a great save.

The whistle blew. We ran off the field for a line change.

"Good job," said Derkie. "Just keep shooting." Then he patted me on the back. "Great job getting around your d-man. Took a lot of power."

Three weeks into my testosterone cycle and there was a noticeable difference in my strength. I could feel it; Derkie could see it. "Weights are paying off," I said. I squirted water in my mouth. "We can score next shift, but Spooner needs to get to the net."

My next shift out, we wanted to execute a similar play on the attack, only this time Derkie had instructed Spooner to drive the net harder. When I saw my d-man coming at me, I held up my stick, bracing to hit him. With my added strength, I wanted to stand up for once and be the player who could lay a great cross-check.

He came at me. So I went at him. And I didn't back down, nor did I roll or dodge or use my quick feet to move by him. I braced my body and let him come.

He was well over two hundred pounds.

I gritted my teeth and smashed my stick against his body. His body wavered for a second. I'd never made a big guy lose his balance. Before he could nail me back, I grunted and hit him again. This time he stumbled, so I dodged around him. He swung at me, clipping me in the thigh. The pain shot through my body. But I kept moving, and manoeuvred by him to snag a pass out of the air. In the clear, I saw the top corner. I wound up, and using every ounce of my body weight, whipped the ball.

It sunk to the back of the net.

We high-fived and raced off the field for a line change.

When I hit the sidelines, Blackie came up to me and asked, "You need ice?"

I sat down on the bench and Blackie lifted the leg of my shorts. A big red welt had surfaced on my thigh. He placed the ice on my leg.

"Thanks." I tried to make eye contact but couldn't because Blackie was staring at my leg, my newly developed thigh muscle, and he had this puzzled look on his face. Immediately I took the ice pack from him. "It's not that bad," I said. "Nothing I can't handle. I can ice it. You go check everyone else. I'm going to be back out soon anyway."

When Blackie looked me in the eyes, I wanted to shrink into the dirt. He was obviously searching for an answer to something. Was he putting two and two together? He was a trainer and had studied muscles.

"I've been hitting the gym hard," I mumbled. "And bulking up with protein." I placed the ice on my thigh and pulled the leg of my shorts over the ice pack.

Fortunately I was saved by Derkie's booming voice. "Moore, you ready?"

I tossed the ice aside. I'd played with bruises before.

At the half, we were down by one. I was totally frustrated with my teammates. They weren't giving enough to get us the win, and my scholarship was riding on their play. I got them in a circle. "This is not good enough! We're not hitting or taking the big hits. Everyone needs to work harder. Let's get physical and pound the crap out of them. And get to the net to score. We can do this!"

Most of the guys cheered, but I noticed some hung their heads. Why would they do that? Body language was important. You let the opposing team see a weakness and you were doomed.

My first shift out, I nailed a guy so hard he crashed to the ground and dropped the ball. I scooped it up and drilled a pass off to Hambone, who immediately wound up for a shot. But he shot straight at the goalie. The whistle blew. As we ran off, I said, "Pick your spots. Don't just shoot. Focus and aim."

"I know. Okay." He shook his head at me.

Every time I was out, I tried to score, but my linemates just weren't there for me. By the end of the game, I knew I'd played hard and strong but my team hadn't. We lost 5–4. I was mad. I'd bounced off checks, but more than that, I'd made a few solid bodychecks myself, knocking guys off the ball, creating turnovers.

I took off my helmet and sweat dripped down my face. Derkie approached me. "That's the strongest I've seen you play," he said. "You've always been tough but tonight you battled back big time."

Normally I liked it when Derkie told me I played well, but tonight it made me uncomfortable. I wanted the conversation off me. "Too bad no one else played tough," I snapped.

Derkie tilted his head and gave me a funny look. "It's okay to be angry, but learn from the loss. I thought some guys played well. Walker was hitting hard. Hamilton created offence. And let's face it, their goalie made a few key saves. For what it's worth, that's the best I've seen *you* play." He paused. "How much weight have you put on?"

"Ten," I lied. "I've been hitting the gym. Just working on legs and guns."

He patted me on the back. "I told John Markham you were a hard worker in the gym."

"I bet Syracuse doesn't talk to me after tonight though. Not after we lost."

"If they don't, you'll get another shot. Hit the showers."

I walked to the change room by myself as I was the last one on the field. I could have secured something tonight if my teammates had pulled through. Damn. I could have been done with the testosterone. The longer I was on it, the more time there was for someone to figure it out, and Blackie was close, I could tell. Was Derkie too? He'd noticed my weight gain.

I fumed all the way across the field. When I entered the dressing room, Hambone was already undressed and ready to hit the showers. I threw my helmet into my bag, then turned to face my team. Suddenly just looking at some of them acting like nothing had happened made my blood boil.

"What was that?" I yelled. "We played like a bunch of babies. We let them beat us."

"Nathan, relax," whispered Quinn.

I flashed him a look. "Relax! Relax? Are you kidding me? We just got the shit beaten out of us and you want me to relax?" We'd failed. We'd lost. I hated losing. And now I would have to wait even longer for my scholarship.

"We are a better team than them!" I went on. "How could you guys just give up?" I saw Jimmy look away and that made me even madder. "Geez, Spooner, at least you could have gone to the net. And, Duncan — Walker was hitting but where were you tonight?"

"He hit," retorted Walker. "I was out there with him." He tossed his towel over his shoulder and picked up his shaving kit. "I don't need this. I'm *hitting* the showers."

"I'm captain and I'm talking! No one hits the showers. Their goalie shut us down. Beaulieu, you lost the game for us by letting in two weak goals."

Suddenly the door creaked and Derkie walked in. The room fell silent. I tried to catch my breath. My anger dissipated and I felt as if it was seeping through my feet and into the floor. I had been a captain of many teams and had never talked to my teammates like that, had never singled guys out.

Derkie frowned and looked at everyone. "What's going on in here?"

"Why don't you ask your captain?" Walker strode past Derkie to the showers. At least the sound of the water running was a little noise.

"Moore, see me outside," said Derkie.

My stomach ached and I wanted to throw up. I heard the door slam behind Derkie and I got up. Ignoring the stares, I stepped over scattered equipment and headed outside. Derkie was leaning against the brick wall.

As soon as he saw me, he straightened, stared at me, and said, "What was that all about?"

"No one worked tonight."

"It's not your place to single guys out. I heard the comment you made to Beaulieu. That's not your job as captain. I'm the coach."

I tried to speak but my throat was parched and I couldn't get any words out.

"If I ever hear you do that again, I'll take the C away from you." Then he turned and walked away.

I re-entered the dressing room and headed to my stall without looking at anyone. By now, most of the guys were in the shower. I sat down, leaned my head back, and closed my eyes.

"Who's up for Earl's downtown?" I heard Hambone ask the team.

Most of the guys said they wanted to go. I didn't answer.

I must have sat with my eyes closed for almost ten minutes, because when I finally opened them, most of the guys were dressed and ready to take off. Hambone was putting on his jacket. I took off my kidney protector and tossed it into my bag. Then I took off my dry-fit undershirt. I leaned over to get my towel out of my bag.

"What's with your back?" Hambone asked.

I immediately sat up and leaned against the wall so my back wasn't exposed. "I broke out bad," I said. "I think I'm allergic to the soap my mom's buying."

"I had a reaction like that once from some perfumed soap my mom bought," he said. "She gave me allergy pills and it went away."

From across the room I could feel someone staring at me. When I looked up, Ryan quickly glanced away. I turned to Hambone and attempted a smile. "Thanks for the tip," I said.

"No problem." He stood and glanced at Spooner. "You ready?"

Spooner nodded without looking at me.

I had two towels in my bag so I wrapped one around

my waist and the other one around my shoulders. In the shower, I made sure my back was to the wall. By the time I was done, everyone had gone but Ryan. He sat on the bench, fully dressed.

"You gotta get control." He talked in a low voice.

"I know." I towelled my hair.

"That was bad."

"I said I know." I put on my dress pants.

"Seems to be working though," he said. "You've beefed up and made your game better."

"Yeah." I had my back to him but I knew he was staring at my bigger torso. I quickly threw on my shirt before I turned to face him.

"Listen," he said, looking toward the door, then back at me, "I'm going to start selling the stuff. After this cycle, you can buy off me."

I buttoned my shirt. "I'm only doing one." I tucked my shirt in my pants and gathered up my things, throwing my tie in my pocket.

"I bet you change your mind. I've also got some other stuff if you ever need anything."

I glared at him. "Dude, I don't do drugs. Never have and never will. And I told you, I'm only doing one cycle of this." I narrowed my eyes. "Were you the one who brought the uppers to my house party last Christmas?"

"This can't get out," he stated. "We'll *both* be done. In different ways of course." He smirked. "Control your side effects."

After Ryan left the dressing room, I sat on the bench and put my head in my hands. As captain, I should say something to Derkie about Ryan, because that was my job. But I couldn't because Ryan was right, I was involved. What the hell else was he selling?

I rubbed my temples. I didn't want to know.

Steroids were illegal to traffic but not illegal to have personally, so I wasn't doing anything criminally wrong. But as an athlete, I was definitely cheating the system. That was what Ryan had meant by us both being done in different ways. He could be criminally charged but I would be morally guilty.

That would hurt my scholarship chances. And maybe get me kicked out of Podium.

Why was I being so stupid?

Yes, I had played well tonight — but at what cost?

On a night when I should feel good about how I played, instead I felt sick to my stomach.

CHAPTER SEVEN

The night was clear, stars shone, and a big full moon lit the sky. My feet felt heavy as I walked to my Jeep. I inhaled, trying to suck in as much fresh air as possible. I kicked stones as I plodded. Closer to my car, I saw Carrie sitting on the back bumper.

"What are you still doing here?" I asked.

"Quinn said you might need a friend." She hopped off the bumper and shoved her hands in her pockets. Then she said, "Tough loss. I hate losing."

"Me too," I said, opening the hatch and throwing in my equipment.

"You want to go get something to eat?" she asked.

I looked at her and attempted a smile. "That sounds good coming from you."

"Yeah, well, we all have our stuff to deal with." She jerked her head toward my car. "Let's take your car. You can drop me back here after."

Carrie got in the front seat and I started the Jeep, letting it warm up for a few seconds. Neither of us said anything. I liked that about Carrie; she knew when to talk and when to shut up. I let the car idle in park and said, "Where would you like to go?"

"Your team is at Earl's."

I sighed. Then I ran my fingers through my wet hair. "Yeah, I know."

"Quinn wants you to come."

"What did he say?"

"Just that you're pissed off your team lost. I get that."

"I flipped out on my teammates." I leaned back, stared at the ceiling of the Jeep, and placed my hands on my forehead. "I can't believe I did that. I've never done it before."

"Ouch," said Carrie. "That's not good. But hey, I've done it. You'll be a bigger man if you show up. It's as good as an apology."

I rolled my head and looked at her. "When did you get so smart?"

She shrugged and gave me a smile.

We drove in silence, and within fifteen minutes we were in Earl's parking lot. Carrie and I entered the restaurant and she whispered, "Chin up, buttercup."

For the first time since the end of the game, I laughed.

We headed to the table where my entire team and some of their girlfriends sat. Two seats were available across from Spooner and his girlfriend, Melanie. I sucked in a deep breath and made my way to the seats. "Hey," I said, sitting down beside Hambone.

"Glad you made it," he said.

Spooner looked at me, nodded slightly, and I gave him a thumbs-up. Carrie was right. Now that I had shown up, all was okay. I opened my menu.

"Hey, have you heard from Allie?" Carrie asked just after the waitress had taken our orders. We had both ordered chili chicken, but I had also ordered dry ribs and calamari for protein. I was starving, and besides, I had to eat a lot to show the guys why I was getting bigger.

I pulled my phone out of my pocket. "I forgot. I'll text her now."

I quickly fired off a text.

"how was your game?"

Within seconds my phone pinged.

"we won 100–81. U?"

I fired another one back.

"how many for u?"

"20. U?"

"bad night."

"where r u?"

"earls with guys"

"eat lots miss you"

"me too"

"So? Did they win?" Carrie asked, her shoulder rubbing up against mine. She moved closer to look at my phone and I felt her breast against my arm. The weight she'd put on after she'd come out of rehab had gone to all the right places. My mouth went dry and I could feel sweat beading on my forehead. My heart picked up its pace and I wanted to touch her.

"Yeah," I answered. I tried to move away from her, but my body wouldn't listen to my brain's command because I really liked the feeling of her breast on my arm. "And she scored twenty points as usual," I said.

Hambone jabbed me in the ribs. "You guys are like the perfect athletic couple."

Of course Carrie had to respond, "Perfect isn't the word for them. Both captains, both top scorers, both —"

I playfully shoulder-checked her, wanting her to stop, knowing my face was as red as a tomato. I had to finish her sentence for her. "Both fans of Jim Carrey. Right?"

"Allie hates Jim Carrey." Carrie did her usual face scrunching, which made me laugh.

Within an hour we had finished eating. Carrie said she needed to get home because she had early practice. We walked to my Jeep and I kept leaning into her, just to be close to her amazing body. Everything about her excited me: her floral perfume, her soft hair, and especially her breasts.

We got in the Jeep, and for the entire drive back to her car, I squirmed in my seat, wishing I could do something about how horny she was making me. I'd never had these kinds of feelings for Carrie before; we'd always been just friends. Were these feelings because of the testosterone?

"Thanks for the lift," said Carrie when we were in the parking lot. "I had fun. Hope you did too." She paused, then glanced at me, her long hair framing her face. I liked it when she wore it long. It made her look so sexy.

"I did." I paused too. "Hey, thanks for listening."

"You didn't say anything, knucklehead."

I laughed. "Okay, then thanks for not saying anything."

She gave me a little punch on the arm and I leaned away from her. I had to. Otherwise I was going to take her in my arms and kiss her hard, and run my hands all over her body.

"Remember to talk to Allie for me, okay?" she said softly.

I gripped the steering wheel. Allie. I could never cheat on Allie; she was too good, too pure. It would hurt her. "Yeah," I said. "I'll talk to her."

Allie came over Sunday when she got home from Edmonton. My parents had gone to Marissa's indoor soccer game way in the south of Calgary. I knew they'd be gone for a good couple of hours. She flopped down beside me on the sofa in the basement and I immediately put my arm around her and started stroking her velvet skin. She leaned her head on my shoulder.

"I have so much homework to do," she moaned.

"Me too," I said, nuzzling her neck with my nose. "But who cares about homework right now?"

"Me," she said. She ran her fingers up and down my chest. "And you should too. Didn't you fail a math test recently?"

"I don't want to talk about math right now," I said.

She touched my arm. Suddenly she stopped, pulled back, and stared at me. "Holy," she said. She wrapped her fingers around my biceps.

I pulled my arm away from her. "I'm sucking back the protein shakes."

"You're really filling out."

"My dad said it's natural for my age." I touched her face, needing to get her off the topic.

I breathed a sigh of relief when she snuggled against me again, laying her head on my chest. Where Carrie smelled like perfume, Allie smelled like soap. I slowly lay back on the sofa, taking Allie with me. We were curled up, side by side, and when she turned her head to look at me, I kissed her. Within seconds my body reacted. Everything inside me was on fire and bursting.

I wanted to touch her, feel her skin. I put my hand under her shirt. We'd hardly done anything in four months, so maybe today was the day. I let my hand move slowly up her stomach until I hit her bra. It fit her like a glove, so I manoeuvred my hands around to her back to get at the clasp. I managed to undo it on the first try. Then I slowly moved my hands back to her front, sliding them underneath the now-loose bra. When I touched her breast, I had to suck in a deep breath.

I reached down and started to undo the zipper on her jeans. Her warm hand covered mine. "No," she murmured.

"Why?" I whispered.

"I dunno."

"Come on, Allie," I whispered in her ear. "My parents won't be home for a while. We've got lots of time."

She put her hands under my shirt and lifted it enough so that our torsos touched. Her warm skin against mine made me moan. "You feel so good," I said in her ear.

We kissed for a few more minutes and then I put my hand on the fly of her jeans again. I wanted her entire body naked beside mine. Long legs, flat stomach, perfect hips.

"No," she said, moving my hand again.

"Why not?" I whispered. "We've been together for almost five months now." I kissed her arched neck. "It'll be okay."

Suddenly I felt her body shift and she sat up and pulled her shirt down. "Nathan, I said no."

I blew out a rush of air, stood, and held up my hands.

"Where are you going?" she asked.

"I gotta take a shower. I can't take the teasing." I stalked off to the bathroom and slammed the door behind me.

The cool water streamed over my body, calming it. What was wrong with me? My mother had taught me that when a girl says no, she means no, and that is all there is to it. I shouldn't have said that about the teasing. I wondered if she'd gone home. I turned the shower off and listened.

I dried myself off, quickly pulled on shorts, and went back to the rec room. No Allie. I closed my eyes and pounded my head with my fists.

Then I heard the front door opening.

I took the stairs three at a time, pulling my T-shirt over my head, and ran outside just as she was getting into her car. I grabbed her door and yanked it open.

"Allie, I'm sorry."

She tried to pull the door shut on me but I kept holding it open.

"I'm really, really sorry."

"You've changed, Nathan."

"No, I haven't," I said. "I can't help it if you make me crazy."

She let go of the door and her shoulders slumped. "I'm just not ready, Nathan." She started to cry. "And I don't know why."

"It's okay. Don't cry."

"I . . . I'm so sorry I was a tease."

I lifted her face with my finger. Then I wiped away her tears. "You weren't. This was my fault. My mom taught me that when a girl says no, I should respect that."

She looked at me and attempted a smile. "That mom of yours, she's one smart cookie."

"I know." I stroked her hair. "Super-smart," I whispered, "just like you." I paused for a second, then waggled my eyebrows up and down. "You want to go for something to eat, bottomless pit?"

One corner of Allie's mouth lifted and she shook her head. "Why is it so friggin' hard for me to stay mad at you?" Then she looked me straight in the eyes. "And I want to, y'know, stay mad."

"I know," I said softly.

She tilted her head, gazed at me for a few seconds, then said, "I want pizza. Pepperoni and mushrooms."

"I hate mushrooms."

"I know that."

That night when I was finally in bed, I stared at the dancing shadows on the walls and thought about what had happened. Was my urge to have sex with Allie because of the testosterone? But Allie and I were seniors in high school and had been together almost *five months*. I squeezed my eyes shut. It was natural to want sex at my age. And she was beautiful and amazing as a person.

Then I thought about Carrie. Now that, I decided, was probably the testosterone because I'd never been attracted to Carrie in that way before.

I rolled over. Allie and I had gone for pizza and patched

things up — but had we really? We'd been fighting a lot lately, ever since she started spending time with that Parm chick. If she knew I was injecting, we would be done for sure; she'd questioned my new-found biceps.

If only we'd beaten the Hamilton Vipers, then I'd have my scholarship and I could quit. The testosterone *was* working for me physically and I liked the muscle-building part, but I hated the lying and the secrecy and the side effects. We had another big game coming up. Maybe that would be my big break.

Not much longer, Nathan. Just get a school to commit, then you can quit.

CHAPTER EIGHT

I looked down at the syringe. I was halfway through the cycle. Only five weeks to go. What if I didn't have my scholarship by the end of the ten weeks? I didn't want to do another cycle.

Our next lacrosse game had come and gone, and we'd won and I'd scored three goals, but still not a word from Syracuse.

I grabbed the flesh of my thigh and jabbed it with the needle. Once the needle was all the way in, I pulled it back just a little. I did the same thing every time. When I saw no blood, I plunged in the syringe and immediately pulled it out.

And that's when it happened. Blood started squirting from the puncture, gushing like a fountain. I put my hand on my thigh to stop it and the blood seeped through my fingers.

I looked down. The sheets on my bed were now stained red.

"Crap. Crap. Crap."

I quickly looked around. I needed something to stop

it. A towel. T-shirt. Anything to apply pressure to my leg. There was a towel lying on the floor on the other side of the room. I limped over and snatched it off the floor and put it to my thigh, pressing it against my skin.

Why was there blood? I'd checked the needle. There'd been no blood in it.

I sat back down on my bed and stared at the blood-ied towel. I waited a few more minutes before I took the towel off to have a look. I exhaled when I saw blood was no longer squirting. Suddenly I realized that I was really trembling. I could taste fear in my mouth.

Should I phone Terry?

Or Ryan? He was a teammate.

I found my phone and was just about to punch in Ryan's number when I stopped myself. I didn't want him knowing anything about me because I didn't want to be sucked further into his shady world. I threw my phone down on the bed.

Instead I logged on to my computer. My heart was beating like mad as I read page after page, trying to find my answer. I scrolled and scrolled. It took me a few sites before I found it.

"I must have nicked a vein," I said out loud. "If I had injected into it, I would feel nauseous."

I put my hand on my thigh. I *had* checked the syringe. There'd been no blood in it. The needle must have passed through a vein and that was why there wasn't any blood when I pulled it back. The good news was that if I just passed *through* it, I wouldn't have injected *into* it. Injecting into a vein or artery could cause a blood clot in the heart.

All the juice would still have been injected into my muscle. I squeezed my eyes shut and breathed a sigh of relief. I put my hand to my heart anyway and tried to feel its beat. It seemed okay.

This was stupid. What was I doing to myself?

I opened my eyes and that was when I saw the bloodied towel on the floor. What would I tell my mother? I had a cut. Then I saw my sheets. They were bloody too. And my hands. I had to wash them.

I stripped the bloody sheets off my bed and shoved them into my closet. Then I ducked into my bathroom and had a quick shower. Once I was dried, I took clean sheets from the shelf. If my parents heard me, they would wonder why I was changing my sheets at midnight. I never changed sheets at all.

Once the clean sheets were on my bed, well, sort of on my bed, I crawled between them and tossed and turned for at least an hour before I fell into a fitful sleep.

My alarm went off at 8:00 a.m., and I moaned. I did not want to get up.

In a blur I showered and dressed, then went upstairs, grabbed a granola bar, and left for school. I slept through first period and tried to sleep through second, but we were working on a project so I had to stay awake.

Finally the day was over and I headed to the dressing room. A good hard practice would wake me up. I quickly got in my gear, and once outside, I broke into a sprint. Partway around the field, my leg started to hurt where I had done the injection the night before. Next injection,

I would have to try my shoulder. I'd just slowed down to give my leg a break when I heard someone coming up behind me. Thinking it was Hambone, I turned. But it was Blackie.

"You okay?" he asked.

"Yeah, I'm good. Just need to stretch a bit before sprinting full out."

"You're learning." He squeezed my shoulder.

For some reason I pulled away from him. I guess I just didn't want him touching my muscles, feeling how big they now were.

He gave me a puzzled look. "Shoulder sore?"

"A little," I lied. "I took that big hit."

"Come see me after. I'll give you a quick massage."

Everyone on the team loved it when Blackie gave massages. "Sure," I said. Then I started running again, making my way to the rest of my team. I had to suck it up and pretend nothing was wrong. There was no way I would go see him for a massage, no way I would take off my shirt and let him see my newly formed body. And my backne. Not a chance.

After warm-up we were put with our lines to work on an offensive drill. I jogged on the spot, waiting for our turn. When Derkie tossed the ball our way, then blew the whistle, I ran toward it because it was closest to me. I scooped it up and ran toward the net. I saw Walker on defence and he was coming at me. I wasn't afraid of him anymore, and I cradled my stick, working it back and forth. Spooner sprinted to the net and Hambone weaved behind me. Once Walker was in front of me, I used my quick feet to fake him out, then I rolled and spun, sending a pass back to Quinn, who immediately passed it off. Spooner was in front of the net and he snagged it and took a shot. Beaulieu made the save just as Walker nailed me with a cross-check. I knew the play was over, but I turned and pushed him right back. He frowned at me. "Play's over, dude." He gave me a little jab.

I clenched my stick, then rammed my body into his torso. Winded, he grabbed his stomach, stumbled, and fell. Even *I* knew it had been a dirty hit.

"Hey, what's going on over there?" yelled Derkie. "Moore, cut the cheap shots."

Walker glared at me when he got up. "What is your problem? We're on the same team." He shook his head at me.

When practice ended, Derkie shouted, "Hit the gym!"

Our workout was on the board and I paired up with Hambone. Most of the exercises were fast foot movements and conditioning-type exercises. After an hour we were both dripping sweat. Everyone picked up their gear to hit the showers.

"You want to stay and do some strength work?" Hambone asked me. "We can spot each other."

"Sure," I replied.

We decided to do chest presses first. I stacked the weights on the bar, then lay down on the bench on my back. I grabbed the bar and easily made the weight. Quinn added more. Again I lifted it no problem. He whistled through his teeth. "You're killing these weights."

"Been working at it," I said quickly.

"You *must* be hitting it hard. You've never lifted this much."

I pushed the weight up, blowing out through my mouth with a loud exhale. After I racked the bar, I sat up. "I want a scholarship and the weights are helping me get some mass."

"Impressive," he said.

"Thanks," I replied without looking at him. Then I stood up. "Your turn."

"You've *really* bulked," he said.

"I tell you, it's the protein shakes."

He gave me a funny look and I wondered if I was just getting paranoid.

It was around six when I walked through the garage door that led into the kitchen. Both my mom and dad were in the kitchen getting dinner ready. My dad liked to cook as much as my mother did.

"Hi, Nathan," said my mom.

"Yo."

"How was your day?" She asked the same question every day.

I shrugged. "I'd like to say another day, another dollar, but that ain't the truth. Practice was okay, school boring."

"I found an English assignment you handed in," said my dad. "You only got fifty-three percent. That's just not good enough. Your grades are important for a scholarship."

"What assignment?" I glared at him. Why was he going through my things? Had he been in my room?

"It looked like a quiz about a novel."

"It's worth like point zero, zero, *zero* five." I really wasn't into talking about school with my father so I started to head down to my room.

"I did your laundry today," said my mother. "I picked up the blood-stained sheets that were in your closet. What happened?"

I froze. Had she been in my room too? Did she go in my drawers? That little drawer where my stash was? Did she find everything? A sudden shot of something that was almost electrical surged through my body. I hated that my parents thought they could just go in my room anytime they wanted. If I was at a billets' they wouldn't do that. I spun around to face my mom. "Why are you always snooping in my room?"

"I wasn't snooping." She looked taken aback. I never yelled at my mother, ever.

"You're lucky she does your laundry," snapped my dad.

"She doesn't have to go through my room! And neither do you. I hate that."

"She wouldn't have to if you would bring your clothes up. And I wouldn't have to if I could trust you to do your homework." He frowned at me. "Why *were* your sheets all bloody?"

"None of your business!"

"Why won't you just answer the question?"

"Because I don't want to! And I don't have to."

My dad stepped toward me, his nostrils flaring. "It is our business while you live under our roof."

"Maybe I got a paper cut."

"Okay. What was so hard about saying that?" I could tell he knew I was lying.

"I told you already. I hate it when you guys go through my room!" I was really yelling now. "That's why it was so hard!"

"What's going on in here?" Marissa had come out from her bedroom.

I spun to face her. "Shut up! No one invited you into this conversation."

"Why are you so crabby?" She held one of my video games in her hand. "Here," she said. "I borrowed this."

I snatched it out of her hands. "Were you in my room too?"

I balled my empty hand into a fist and glared at her. She stepped back when I raised it to her face and she looked as if she might cry. Her eyes were wide and she honestly looked scared of me.

"Nathan, don't threaten your sister like that," commanded my father.

"Here we go again." I held up my hands. "Let's stick up for the little turd and blame Nathan for everything. She was in *my* room!"

"We're not blaming you for anything," said my mother softly.

"No!? Well, that's what it seems like to me."

My dad stepped closer to me. "Don't you dare speak to your mother like that. She never raises her voice to you."

My body started shaking and I knew I had to get downstairs and away from this conversation. I had to get myself under control. This was crazy. I started to move toward the door when my father put his arm on my shoulder. "We're not finished here. You need to apologize to your mother. And your sister."

Just the touch of his hand on my shoulder did something to me and I shoved him away. I must have caught him off guard because he stumbled. I heard my sister gasp and saw my mother put her hand to her mouth. This was the same reaction I'd had on the field today with Walker. I had to get to my room.

I started to head to the door, but my father grabbed my T-shirt at the neck and yanked me toward him. We were almost touching noses when he hissed, "Don't you ever push me again." His narrowed eyes told me I had crossed the line.

Behind me, Marissa started to sniffle. "Don't fight," she whimpered.

"You're ripping my T-shirt," I said. I jerked away from him.

He put his hand on my upper arm. He was going to say something, I knew he was, but then the look on his face changed from anger to shock as his fingers pressed into my muscle. I slowly pulled away from him. No jerk, no yank.

I looked at my mother and said, "I'm sorry, Mom." Then I said, "And sorry too, Marissa."

My dad said nothing more and I rushed to the stairs. I was shaking so hard I had to grab the hand railing to get downstairs. Once I was in my room, I shut the door and leaned against it. Then I sank to the floor and curled into a ball, resting my forehead on my knees.

Nothing about my outburst was mentioned during dinner. I have to admit that shocked me. I was waiting for my dad to say something, anything, and it must have been killing him to keep his mouth shut. And my mother didn't say anything either. We ate dinner and surface-talked. Even Marissa was quiet, and that had to be a first. After dinner I helped Mom with the dishes but we barely spoke. When the dishes were done, she simply said thanks.

Down in my room, I waited for the footsteps.

But no one came down. I think that made it worse because I was left alone to think, and my mind wouldn't shut off. They knew. They had to know. Two hours went by before I finally heard the footsteps and I assumed it was my father. He would be the one to have The Talk with me.

"Nathan?" My mom's voice came from the other side of the door.

Surprised, I sat up. "Come in."

She slowly opened the door and then she just stood in the door frame for a second. When she looked at me, she tried to smile. "I just wanted to see if you were okay." Her voice was soothing and compassionate.

"I'm fine," I said.

She moved into my room and sat on the end of the bed. "Is there anything you want to talk about?"

My throat went dry. I could feel tears under my eyelids. Why couldn't I talk? Had my father mentioned something to her? Did she want me to come clean about the testosterone? Was she here to give me the opportunity to actually say something before something was said to me?

I ran my hands through my hair and tried to open my mouth. I wanted to tell her, I really did. *Just do it, Nathan. Speak.*

I swear the words were in my throat and ready to come

out when my mom asked, "Is it Allie? Is that why you're out of sorts?"

Allie? Did they think Allie was the reason I was so moody?

"A little," I answered slowly.

She picked at the lint on my comforter. "She's your first real girlfriend, so there'll be a lot to learn. Relationships aren't always easy."

"Girls are complicated," I said.

She laughed. "Yes, your father says that all the time. She's your first too. And she probably won't be your last."

"We've been fighting a lot lately."

My mom nodded. "Yes, that can make you irritable."

"Sometimes I don't think we're suited for each other."

"You're young, Nathan. You don't have to have a girl-friend."

I nodded. Then I said, "Is Dad coming down to talk to me too?"

She tenderly touched my cheek. "No. He left this up to me. He figures I'm better at the relationship talks."

"Okay," I said, attempting a smile. I paused before I added, "I'll be back to normal soon."

"I know," she said. "It's hard being a teenager." She smiled and hugged me. Then she got up and left.

I flopped back on my bed. Wow, lucky break. My mind skipped through my day and I saw Blackie's face and Hambone's, and I could hear Derkie asking me how much weight I'd gained. How much longer could I fool them all? Allie too, and my parents.

My heart sank. I closed my eyes. Not long. I had just

dodged a bullet. But next time it wouldn't be so easy.

I had to stop the injections. Get clean. If I got caught, I would never get a scholarship. If I went off them and no one found out, I still had a chance.

I would keep my secret a secret, get off the juice, and no one would have to know anything.

CHAPTER NINE

First thing I did when I got up was yank out my stash from its hiding place and throw it in a big plastic bag. Then I tied the top of the bag in a knot and stuffed it in my backpack. I didn't care how much it cost or how much money I was wasting. No more. I would do the post-cycle therapy to get back to normal and that was it.

I sat on the end of my bed and rocked back and forth. What I had done made me sick to my stomach. It was wrong, so wrong. Cheating was never the way to go. Could I continue playing as well as I had been without the extra muscle? It had definitely stepped up my game.

I stood up. I could and I would because I had to.

I was so deep in thought on the drive to school that I forgot to throw the plastic bag in the garbage. I would take care of it when I had taken care of something else.

Once at school, instead of going to class, I went to see Blackie in the Podium training room. All the trainers from all the sports worked out of the same room. He was the only trainer in the room when I got there though. Tomorrow was a Professional Development day for the teachers, so many athletes were away at tournaments and meets.

"Sorry I didn't come see you last night," I said.

Blackie was folding towels. He liked all the edges to be perfect. "That's okay," he said. He looked over at me. "How's the shoulder?"

"It's fine. I think it was just a bit stiff."

He turned away from me and continued his folding. "You've put on a lot of mass in a short time," he said.

"I've been drinking a lot of shakes."

He stopped moving and made direct eye contact. The look in his eyes made me want to climb in a hole.

"You're a good kid, Nathan," he said. "You'll get a scholarship because you're a hell of a lacrosse player." He paused and I wondered if he had me figured out.

I couldn't speak.

"Be smart about your future." There was a knock on his door and another Podium athlete came in, looking for ice.

I left because there was nothing more to say.

I acted cool as I walked down the hall, even though my heart raced. Once I figured I was out of sight from everyone, I picked up my pace and jogged out the school's front entrance. Nearby I saw a big green garbage can. I looked around, and when I saw I was alone, I pulled out the plastic bag and shoved it deep into the can. Then I broke into a full sprint to my Jeep. I jumped in, started the engine, and peeled out of the parking lot. Within fifteen minutes I was parked in front of Rocky's.

The doorbell rang when I entered and, sure enough, Terry was behind the front counter. There was no one else in the store.

"Hey," he said, looking up. "How can I help you, kid?"

"I'm done."

He crossed his arms over his chest, which was hard for him to do because of the size of his pecs. "Sure about that? What are you — like halfway through your cycle?"

"Yeah."

"Is it working?"

"Yeah. But it's not me."

He casually leaned back against the counter. "What's happening?"

"I hate the side effects."

He grinned. "My first cycle, I loved them. It was all about girls and sex. I couldn't get enough."

I shifted my stance. I was not comfortable talking to this guy about my sex life or lack of it, and I certainly was *not* interested in hearing about his.

He laughed again, obviously amused by my discomfort. "Ahh. So your girlfriend turned you down."

"Shut up," I said.

"Irritable too, I see. Listen, kid, it's your choice what you do. You could lose some of the muscle you gained if you quit now."

"I don't care. Do I need the post-cycle therapy?"

He nodded. "Yeah, you'll need the PCT. You've got to wean yourself off the juice and get your own testosterone running again. He crossed his arms. "I wouldn't quit, but it's your choice."

"If I stop now, when will it be out of my system?" Questions were piling up in my brain.

He laughed and uncrossed his arms. "Takes a month or so. Maybe more."

I backed up a step. The guy was starting to bug me with his condescending attitude. "Can I get the PCT from you?" There was no way I was going to Ryan for any of this.

"Sure. Pop by the house tonight with two hundred dollars cash."

I left the store confused and angry, and I wished I could just go to my father and ask his advice. He'd know more than that idiot. I wished I'd never started.

I slammed my hands on the steering wheel, over and over, until my palms were red.

When I got back to the school, two cop cars were sitting out front. The policemen were standing at the front door of the school . . . by the garbage can. My stomach tightened and my head started to pound. I parked the Jeep, grabbed my phone, and texted Carrie. I was supposed to be in English class. For some reason, I didn't want to text Allie or anyone from my team. Carrie was the safest.

"whats with cops?"

"u don't know?"

"no"

"ryan duncan got busted"

"for what?"

"drugs"

I slid down in my seat, tilted my head back, and stared upwards. Ryan Duncan arrested? What if he told everyone about me? I'd never bought off him. Still, he could say I *had* bought from someone he knew. What kind of drugs had he sold? I heard the ping on my phone. It was Carrie, asking why I wasn't in English. I fired back a text to say I had a doctor's appointment.

I took a deep breath and got out of the car. My legs shook as I walked. The cops were still outside, standing by the garbage can where I'd thrown that plastic bag. Beads of sweat rolled down my face. *You did nothing illegal, Nathan. Wrong in the sport world, yes, but illegal, no.*

My heart beat like crazy as I walked past them. The lid was on the garbage can. I tried to saunter and act completely cool, but inside, I was like a volcano ready to erupt. They didn't notice me because they were deep in conversation with the principal of the school. I didn't see my plastic bag in their hands. Was I being paranoid?

Heart still racing, I entered the school and looked at my phone to see what time it was. There were only thirty minutes left in the block. No matter what I had done, I was still the captain of my team, and I needed to visit Derkie to see exactly what had happened with Ryan. It was my job.

His office door was shut. I put my ear to the door but I didn't hear any voices. I knocked softly. No answer. I waited a few more seconds before I knocked again. When again there was no answer, I tried the doorknob, but it was locked.

I turned to walk away when I saw him coming down the hall, shoulders slouched.

"Nathan," he said. He sounded exhausted.

"Hey, Derkie."

He unlocked his door and ushered me in. "Have a seat."

I did as he asked. He sat across from me and picked up a pen, which he tipped back and forth and stared at. "I guess you've heard," he said at last.

"I was at a doctor's appointment this morning so I don't know a lot of details."

He put the pen down. Then he ran his hand over his face, exhaled, and shook his head. "It's been challenging to say the least." Derkie clasped his hands, leaned forward, and looked at me. "About a month ago I talked to Ryan because I was suspicious of steroid use. I wanted to help him because everyone deserves a second chance. But he denied it. So I thought I would just watch him closely. That's why I made him an assistant captain. After confronting him, I wanted to see if he would take what I said to heart and make some changes."

He leaned back in his chair and exhaled loudly. I remained quiet.

After a few beats he continued, "In our society, people are innocent until proven guilty. Funny thing was" — he drummed his fingers on his desk — "just yesterday, I had made up my mind to have his urine tested by a doctor. But now I won't have to do that because this morning he was caught selling ecstasy to a kid in the schoolyard." He sighed and shook his head. "I had no idea he was into selling crap like that."

"What will happen to him?"

"I don't know. I met with the police. He has no priors, and he didn't have a lot in his possession. I guess they searched his billets' home too and they didn't find anything. At this point they're interested in finding out who he got the ecstasy *from*." Derkie rubbed his temples.

I ran my fingers up and down my jeans. "I guess we're minus one defence now."

"And a good one too," replied Derkie. "He'll be gone from Podium, and now he's got a criminal record." He looked up and shook his head. "How stupid could he be? He had so much going for him. I've watched him play for years, and pro was definitely in his future."

Neither of us spoke for a few moments and the room took on an eerie silence.

"Well, I should go," I said. I hoped he couldn't hear the tremor in my voice. I stood to leave but didn't actually move.

I opened my mouth to speak, to fess up and tell Derkie everything, because I so wanted to tell someone, but his phone rang.

"I've got to get that," he said.

I left without saying goodbye.

CHAPTER TEN

Derkie's words rang through my mind all day and I walked the halls in a daze. He knew about Ryan, had confronted him, and then given him a second chance. Should I fess up before he confronted me too? Obviously he would figure it out. He had with Ryan. I wanted to tell him first. It was the right thing to do. Unlike Ryan, I would take the second chance.

The buzz in the dressing room before practice was all about Ryan. I didn't add anything to the conversation and dressed in silence.

I had just snapped my helmet in place when Spooner said, "I heard they found a syringe and 'roids in the garbage can."

I almost gasped out loud.

"I heard that too," said Hambone. He stood up, ready to hit the field. "But I also heard it means nothing to the cops because it was just steroids." He walked to the door and I followed. "That stuff could have been put there by anyone," he said. "Our gym is used by some heavy lifters."

Spooner pushed the door open. "Yeah, steroids are small

potatoes when they got someone with ecstasy. But I'm sure we'll get the steroid lecture at school one of these days."

"Let's run," I said.

I took off at a sprint and Spooner and Hambone followed. By the time we reached the field, I was panting. At practice Derkie told the team the news about Ryan Duncan. He didn't use a lot of words but said Ryan was off the team and gone from Podium. Then he worked our butts off and I liked that. It burned some of my nervous energy.

After practice I wanted to talk to Derkie, but he left the field before our last drill, with his phone stuck to his ear and his head down.

Not the right time, I thought. *He's stressed and doesn't need any more stress right now.* I would talk to him later, even tomorrow. I could text him and hook up before practice.

"You going to Jax's tonight?" Hambone asked as we walked to the dressing room.

"Yeah," I said. Jax was having a get-together and going out would take my mind off everything — and get me away from brooding in my room. "See you there."

When I picked up Allie, I immediately saw she looked fantastic. Instead of high-top runners, she wore little-girl-type flat shoes that sparkled. Her hair was totally straightened, and when I got close to her, I was sure she wore perfume.

"You look great," I said as we walked down the front steps.

She tilted her head and smiled. "Thanks," she murmured. "Glad you like."

"What's not to like?" I took her hand in mine, then

lifted it to my lips and kissed her knuckles.

As she was doing up her seat belt, she said, "That is so crazy about Ryan Duncan, that player on your team."

I pulled away from the curb. "Yeah. He's gone from Podium."

"And so he should be." She glanced at me. "I bet he's the one who brought stuff to your party last year."

"I'm not going to accuse him," I said, "because I don't know for sure."

"He for sure did steroids," she said.

"We don't know that either," I said. "When's your next tourney," I asked, changing the subject.

For the rest of the drive, I avoided all talk about Ryan. When we arrived at Jax's, I parked along the curb and Allie reached for the door handle.

"Before we go in," I said, "I want to kiss you."

She leaned into me and our kiss was tender and warm. When we broke apart, she said, "Later, 'kay?"

"I'll take you up on that offer anytime."

We got out of the car and walked up the sidewalk to the front door. Jax opened it after we rang the doorbell three times.

"Hey," he said, slapping my hand. I put my other hand on the small of Allie's back and guided her through the door, a polite move my mother had taught me.

"Everyone is downstairs," said Jax.

Allie and I headed down. It was just a small gathering, which was great. Bowls of chips and Cheezies were set up all over the room. But more importantly, the pool table had been racked and was ready to go.

"Tourney time," announced Aaron.

Hambone handed me a cue. "Partner."

"Lacrosse rules!" I smacked his hand.

"Hockey rules!" Aaron and Kade did some stupid hockey move that their team had invented, thinking it was cool, but in fact, was really lame.

"Flip to break," said Jax.

"Parm and I play the winners," yelled Allie.

"I don't know how to play pool," moaned Parmita.

"Carrie and I will play whoever," said Jax, "seeing as we're the *individual sports* people. And I don't really care who we play 'cause I'm crappy at pool anyway. How about you, Carrie?"

Carrie hip-checked Jax. "I'm a champ."

Hambone and I won the break. I had just taken my shot when Carrie came to stand beside me. "I need some tips," she said, "for when it's my turn."

"From *moi?*" Then I leaned over and whispered in her ear, "I'll let you in on a secret. I'm a crappy pool player too."

She laughed. "Okay. I won't get a tip from you then."

Her perfume hit me and I realized it was the same stuff Allie had on tonight. Maybe they were chumming around again, although Allie hadn't left Parmita's side since we'd arrived.

"You want a pop?" said Carrie.

"Sure," I said, glancing around the room. Allie and Parmita were across the room by the iPod docker choosing music.

"There's other stuff too," said Carrie. "Jax bought it."

Suddenly Allie yelled, "He's driving!"

Both Carrie and I turned to look at Allie, who was now staring at us instead of selecting music. I frowned. Yeah, I was driving, but did she have to act like my bloody mother?

Hambone nudged me. "Your turn," he said.

I took my shot and groaned when I missed the pocket and the ball banked off the side and flew to the other side. Hambone laughed. "You're brutal."

The game continued and I missed a lot of shots. Quinn played better than I did, but that wasn't enough to give us a victory. Carrie hung around the table to pick up tips from anyone who would give them to her. She wore this tight little T-shirt with a V-neck that showed off some pretty good cleavage. Every time she bent over a little, I got an eyeful. I tried not to look.

Allie and Parm watched the game, but only now and again, because as usual they seemed lost in their own little world — which included ignoring Carrie. This, I think, made Carrie flirt with the guys more. I didn't mind her being at the table.

When Aaron and Kade won, they cheered.

"Who's next on our hit list?" Aaron asked just after he'd sunk his last shot.

I went over to Allie and gave her my cue. "You're up," I said. Then I whispered, "Beat the crap out of 'em, okay?"

"Convenient for you," she said snottily.

Baffled by her comment, I furrowed my brows. Why would she say something like that? I didn't answer because what was I supposed to say to a comment that had nothing to do with anything?

"I'm sure you get it," she said.

"Actually I don't." Irritation began to boil inside me. I counted to myself before I replied under my breath, "Sometimes you make no sense."

"What's that supposed to mean?" she snapped.

Without thinking, I retorted, "You tell me."

"You're blind." Then she turned. "C'mon, Parm, let's play and kick some butt."

Completely at a loss, I shook my head as I watched her walk to the pool table. Parmita put her hand at the small of Allie's back just as I had done earlier.

Carrie and Kade came up and stood beside me, unaware that Allie and I had just had words. The three of us chatted about random stuff until I felt eyes on me.

I glanced over at Allie. She was playing pool but also glaring at me. Suddenly it hit me. Carrie was standing beside me. That was what this was about. I lost and wasn't playing and Carrie wasn't playing either, and Allie thought I'd lost on purpose so I could talk to Carrie.

Maybe her mood would change if she won her pool game. I headed to the table to watch the game, which had become quite exciting and loud.

"I can't believe I missed that," moaned Allie.

I sidled up to her and jokingly whispered, "You just need my help."

She turned and made a face. "I don't need your help. You lost."

I put up my hands and stepped away from her. "Hey, I was just kidding."

When she gave me a little fake-attitude smile, I stuck my hands in my pockets. Allie took her shot, then put down her pool cue and went to the cooler. When she came back, she had some type of vodka cooler and also a pop. She handed the pop to me. "You're driving. My turn tonight."

Allie never drank, so this was totally out of character, but I didn't say anything. Was the pop a gesture that we were okay again? "Thanks," I said.

I flipped the tab and took a swig. The noise escalated as the game continued, and it hit a fevered pitch when Allie sank the last ball to beat Aaron and Kade in an awesome upset.

"We won!" Allie smacked hands with Parmita, who, surprise, surprise, grinned. Allie did a little dance, moving her arms around in a circle. "Oh yeah," she said. "We won."

"I know who I'm putting money on next game," I said.

"Hey, great idea," said Aaron. "Let's take bets."

"I need another drink," said Allie. Carrie flashed me a look and I shrugged. This was so not Allie, but then neither was the perfume, makeup, and shoes. Still, she was having a good time and I was all for that.

The pools balls were racked for the next game and Aaron got out the betting sheet. I bet five on Allie and Parmita.

"I'll put five on Carrie and Jax," said Hambone. "I like underdogs." Then he whispered to me, "And Carrie's so hot."

"That she is," I said.

"I heard that," said Allie.

"So?" I said. "I'm agreeing with him, nothing else."

Carrie and Jax got their cues, and Aaron flipped a coin to

see who'd break the balls. When Carrie and Jax won, Allie laughed and said, "That's not going to help them one bit."

I could tell she was starting to feel the drinks even though she was only on her second. I'd never seen her drink more than a sip. Carrie bent over the pool table and naturally I stared at her cleavage. What guy wouldn't? Then I felt eyes boring through my skull. I looked over and Allie was glaring at me.

My mouth dried.

Allie picked up her drink and swigged it back. When she finished, she wiped her mouth and said, "I need another one."

Quinn leaned in and said in a low voice, "Bet ya five she pukes in your car."

The game took on new meaning because Allie became loud and kind of obnoxious, but no one seemed to care except Carrie. Every time it was Carrie's turn, Allie had something to say to her about how lousy she was. And she was lousy. Everyone laughed at Allie's jabs and Carrie did too, but I could see she was getting really bugged. Finally Allie said something about her boobs getting in the way and I thought Carrie was going to cry.

"Knock it off, Allie," I said. Of all people, Allie knew how hard it had been for Carrie last year. Why would she say something like that?

By now Allie was on her way to being really drunk. She threw down her pool cue and stared at me. "Should I *knock it off* so you can cheat on me with her?" Allie's words were slurred.

"Allie, don't," I said.

"You weren't just with the guys that night at the restaurant. You were with her."

The room went silent. So that's what this was about. Why didn't she tell me this when we were alone? But I knew the answer. She was getting drunk and alcohol made people say things they regretted later.

Carrie ran from the room and headed right to the bathroom, slamming the door. The lock clicked. Quinn whistled through his teeth. Jax asked if anyone wanted to watch a movie. When Carrie didn't come out, Aaron went to the bathroom and rapped on the door.

I clenched my hands into fists. My body shook. My heart thumped. My blood swirled around inside my body. I had to leave. I had to go home and not start a scene. *Leave, Nathan, just leave.*

But I couldn't. My feet felt glued to the floor. "Allie," I said loudly, "why would you say something like that to her?"

"Let's play pool," said Kade. "I'll take over for Carrie until she gets back."

"Yeah, Parm, you're up," said Jax.

"Answer me!" I yelled at Allie.

Hambone grabbed me by the back of my shirt and whispered, "Moore, don't."

I shoved him off.

"I'm leaving!" I snarled at Allie. "Get your own ride home."

I sprinted up the stairs and headed for the front door. I wanted to bang it open, rip it off its hinges. I could hear someone behind me but I didn't stop.

"Nathan, wait!" It was Allie and she was crying.

"Wait for what?" I hollered over my shoulder as I ran across the lawn. "For you to continue *not* to trust me even though I've done nothing?"

I knew she was following me. There was no way I was opening the car door for her. I got in the driver's side and she got in the passenger side.

"I'm sorry," she mumbled. "I do trust you. Honest."

"You sure have a strange way of showing it."

I started the engine and tore away from the curb, driving well over the speed limit. I kept driving but I didn't speak to her. I came to an intersection where I could take the highway back into the city or head down a road that went through the countryside. I decided to take the country road. I was still so wound up that I floored the gas. The speedometer shot up.

"Slow down!" Allie held the dashboard. "Nathan, you're being crazy. Don't."

I knew I should slow down, and normally I would have, but for some reason, I kept my foot on the gas. I was going 120 kilometres an hour in an 80 zone. I pressed the gas even harder.

"Nathan, stop!" Allie started to cry.

Even her tears didn't stop me. "What the hell," I said. "Why did you say that to Carrie? You, of all people. You know how she struggled last year. It was nasty, Allie."

"You're always staring at her." Allie's voice was slurred.

"She's my friend."

"She's prettier than me."

"No, she's not. You've changed since you started hanging out with Parm."

"I know it was mean." Allie slumped in her seat. "And I feel awful. But all guys like the pretty girls."

"I'm going out with *you!* I like *you!*" I gunned the car to 130.

"She ... she'd probably have sex with you," Allie sobbed. "And I wouldn't."

I accelerated to 160.

"Nathan, stop. I'm gonna be sick."

I took my eyes off the road and stared at her. "I've never cheated on you. Ever!"

"Watch out!"

The car swerved and I tried to right it by cranking the wheel, but I'd lost control. We flew off the road and over a ditch, and then I saw the fence in front of me. I tried to brake, but the car scraped the posts. Then it hit something and rolled.

Over and over.

CHAPTER ELEVEN

Glass shattered, tires screeched, and metal scraped. The air bags deployed. The smell of burning rubber hit my nostrils. And gas. Allie screamed and screamed. Her high-pitched wail, coupled with the noise of the car crashing along the fence, was deafening. I let go of the steering wheel and tried to grab her, but I was thrown against the back of my seat. The car bounced one last time before it stopped completely.

The Jeep rattled and hissed.

I looked over at Allie and saw blood gushing from her head. All my anger dissolved.

"No!" I shook her arm. "Allie, talk to me."

She moaned. I had to get her out. Now. And call 911. Where was my phone? I pushed my door and it creaked. I threw my weight against it. It had to open. I shoved and shoved. If I had any pain, I couldn't feel it. Nothing. When I had the door open enough, I crawled outside and over dirt and dried grass, until I could stand. Then I ran around to Allie's side of the car, searching my back pocket for my phone. When I felt it, I yanked it out. "Please work. Please work."

When I saw the light and the screen, I hurriedly punched in 911.

The sky was black. No moon or stars to light my way, and no streetlights either. In the dark, I reached Allie's door. "I've been in an accident," I screamed into the phone.

The dispatcher, a woman, asked questions that I answered at the same time as I frantically tried to open the door. "Help is coming, Allie. Hang in there. Please, Allie, be okay. Be okay."

The women kept telling me to calm down, but I kept yelling at her to get help. I pulled on Allie's door and it wouldn't budge. "I'll get it open, Allie, don't worry."

"Nathan, get me out of here." Her voice trembled in fear. Allie hated closed-in spaces. "You have to get me out of here! Get me out! Get me out!" She pounded on the door and I just wanted to touch her, tell her it would be okay.

Using everything I had, I yanked on the door. Finally I opened it enough to reach in and touch her arm. "Allie."

She rolled her head and looked at me. "You have to get me out, Nathan!" she cried. "I'm suffocating. I can't breathe."

What if her back was hurt and I tried to move her and did something to her? What if I paralyzed her because I did something stupid? But she had turned her head, so her neck was okay. If her neck was okay, I thought I could move her. But I didn't know. *Think, Nathan, think.*

"Nathan!" She started screaming again. "Get me out!"

The hysterical sound of her voice made me pry the door open further. She gasped for breath. Once I had enough room, I put my arm under her legs and carefully inched them toward me. "It's okay, Allie. Move your head again." I spoke quietly.

She turned and looked at me. Her eyes were glassy.

"I'll try to swing you around and bring you out feet first. Is that okay?"

"Yes."

I carefully inched her body toward me. I didn't have much room to move her though. Where was the ambulance? How long were they going to take to get here? I wished they'd hurry up.

"Help is coming," I said. "You're going to be okay, Allie." I had to keep talking to her, keep her talking to me.

She nodded.

"Talk to me, Allie. Let me hear you breathe," I said.

She inhaled and exhaled.

I had her legs turned so that all she had to do was inch her butt forward. "Come on, Allie, you can do this."

She nodded and struggled to inch forward. If I could get her a little closer, she could wrap her arms around my neck and I could pull her out.

"M-maybe I'll just sit here for a few seconds," she said. "I'm a little better with the door open." She sucked in great gulps of air.

"Soon you'll be sitting on the grass." I had to sound positive.

"This is my fault," she wailed. "I drank too much. I feel sick."

"Don't think about anything but getting out of the car." Slowly I pulled her closer to me and closer to the opening in the door. "Do you hurt anywhere?"

"My knee," she gasped.

The bleeding on her forehead looked as if it had stopped. I used the cuff of my hoodie to wipe the blood away. There was a gash, but it wasn't spurting blood.

I heard the sirens in the distance. "Hear that? Help's coming," I said. "You're going to be fine."

Once the police and ambulance arrived, things happened fast. The paramedics had the right equipment to get Allie out in minutes. As soon as she was out, she threw up. The paramedics didn't care. They rushed over and put her on a stretcher and immediately took her to the waiting ambulance. I stood there, watching them take her away, when I felt a hand on my shoulder.

"Are you hurt?"

I didn't think I was, but then I coughed and that was when I felt a sharp jab in my chest. "I might have cracked a rib," I said.

The paramedic pointed to the ambulance. "Let's get you checked out."

I walked with the paramedic over to the ambulance. Inside the brightly lit truck, Allie was lying on a cot with an oxygen mask on her face, and all I could see were her eyes. She looked freaked. The female paramedic looking after her took the blood pressure cuff off her arm. "Blood pressure's fine."

A paramedic checked my eyes with a flashlight, checked my pulse, and took my blood pressure. When he asked me to put my arms over my head, I struggled. "That hurts," I said.

"Okay. I think we'll have them take a closer look at you

at the hospital. All your vitals are good."

From the open door of the ambulance, I saw the cops coming toward the vehicle and I knew they were coming to talk to me.

The first cop got into the ambulance and leaned close. I'm sure he had the nose of a bloodhound when it came to alcohol and was checking me out. "Are you the driver of the Jeep?" he asked.

"Yes sir."

"Have you been drinking?"

I shook my head.

"Is he hurt?" the cop asked the paramedic.

"Nothing life-threatening. We'll have him X-rayed at the hospital."

"I'm okay," I muttered. "I've had cracked ribs before." It was painful to breathe, that was all. "I'm sure I'm okay." I knew I was mumbling, repeating myself, but I was so nervous.

The cop looked at the paramedic and asked, "Can we give him a breathalyzer?"

"Sure. He should be fine."

I followed the police to the cruiser and after breathing into the breathalyzer — which was harder than I thought because of my rib — they put me in the back seat. I looked out the window at the dark night, now lit up like a scoreboard with all the police lights flashing. Only this time it was a horrible game I wasn't even close to winning. Everything seemed surreal, as if I was in a movie and not my own life.

"I hope my girlfriend's okay." I choked on my words.

"She's in good hands," the cop replied. "They'll take both of you to the hospital to be checked out." He was looking down at his paperwork. Without turning to look at me, or even look up, he said, "You have no alcohol in your system. You're lucky." Now he turned to look at me. "But let's talk about how fast you were going."

I tried to swallow.

"Were you speeding?"

I just about replied that I didn't think so, but something stopped me. I looked the policeman in the eyes and said, "Yes. I was."

"I'll have to charge you with reckless driving. And if your girlfriend has any life-threatening injuries, you could also be charged with dangerous driving causing injury."

I didn't say anything. He turned from me and I could hear his pen scratching across the paper as he wrote a report of some sort. I wondered what I'd be charged with. Would I just get a huge fine? Could they charge me with dangerous driving causing injury even if Allie was just a little hurt?

Suddenly it hit me. I had crashed the Jeep and totalled it completely.

"I ... I have to phone my parents," I stammered. I blinked and felt salty tears trickling down my cheeks. I lowered my head and wiped at my cheeks, hoping the cop didn't see.

"We've contacted them already." Again, he didn't look up.

"Are they coming here?" I squeaked.

"We advised them to meet us at the hospital. Your car will be towed to an impound lot."

I rubbed my hands up and down my thighs. "My

girlfriend's parents live in Halifax."

"We've been in touch with the people she lives with in Calgary." He snapped his book shut and looked at me through the rear-view mirror. "Would you like to ride with your girlfriend in the ambulance?"

I nodded.

I held Allie's hand in the ambulance but we didn't talk much. She said she was sorry and I said I was sorry back, but after that I think we were both too stunned to say anything else.

My parents and Allie's billet parents were waiting in Emergency when we arrived. My mother rushed over to me first.

"Nathan, are you okay?" She put her hand on my cheek. I leaned my head a little to feel the warmth of her fingers. Then I stared at the toe of my shoe. "I totalled the Jeep," I said. "I'm so sorry."

My dad stepped forward and gently placed his hand on my shoulder. "That doesn't matter right now. What's important to your mother and me is that you're alive. The police told us you were extremely lucky. They said it could have been a lot worse and they're surprised it didn't end with a fatality. We're glad you're okay."

I nodded before I glanced over at Allie, sitting with her billets. "I hope she's okay," I said. "I think she hurt her knee."

My dad looked at Allie too. "She's got a gash on her forehead, too, but I've seen a lot worse." He turned back to me and said, "She'll be fine."

"I wasn't drinking," I said.

"I know," replied my father, gently patting me on the back. "And, son, that's a good thing."

I didn't deserve the praise, so I changed the subject. "I think I might have a cracked rib. It feels the same as last year when I got injured down in the States."

"They'll have to do an X-ray."

The nurse came out and called Allie's name. I held out my hand for her to touch when she limped by me. "I'll call later, okay?"

She nodded.

I had to wait another twenty minutes before I was called in to see the doctor, who gave me a thorough checking over, including eyes, ears, blood pressure. He also had me lie down and then checked my limbs and internal organs for any soreness. The only thing that came up was the possible cracked rib. The doctor left and immediately my father came into the curtained-off cubicle.

"So," he said.

"I need an X-ray."

Suddenly a cold silence hovered over us. My dad was staring at my shirtless upper body. Then he turned his head and closed his eyes. I immediately picked up my shirt and threw it on. With everything that had happened, I had forgotten about the changes the testosterone had done to my body. My dad was seeing me shirtless for the first time since I'd started injecting. I'd been so careful till now to cover myself up in baggy hoodies and long-sleeved T-shirts.

He put his hand on my shoulder. "Let's get the X-ray done. Your mother is anxious to take you home."

CHAPTER TWELVE

Both Allie and I were released from the hospital just after one o'clock in the morning. When I was home again, I thought I'd never felt more tired and worn out. I downed a painkiller for my rib, said my goodnights, and went down to my room. I curled up under my covers. What a mess I'd made of everything. Allie had been assessed at the hospital and the only thing she'd really injured was her knee, so the cops had decided to charge me with reckless driving, giving me a huge fine and suspending my license for three months. I would have to log mega-hours in Dad's office to pay the fine.

My dad let me know I got off easy.

But even I knew that.

I put my hand on my biceps. My dad hadn't said anything to me about my body, so I didn't know what to think. Had he noticed? Why was all this happening now — now, when I'd decided to quit the juice? I rolled over. I tried to sleep but I just lay there, staring into the dark. Breathing was painful, and shadows bounced all over my room.

I looked at the bedside clock — 3:00 a.m. passed, then 4:00 a.m.

At last I couldn't stand the guilt any longer. I needed to unload on somebody. Without turning on any lights, I got out of bed and crept upstairs, through the kitchen, and down the hall to my parents' bedroom. I stood outside the door for a minute, listening to my father snoring and my mother sighing.

I slowly creaked open the door and stood in the door frame.

My mom popped up right away. "Nathan. What is it? What's wrong, honey?"

"I need to talk to Dad."

Without asking why, she shook my dad's shoulder. "Alan, wake up. Nathan needs you."

My dad slowly lifted his head, propped his upper body on his elbows, and squinted at me. "If you're in pain, take another painkiller."

"Dad, I want to talk to you."

I guess I expected him to say something about it being the middle of the night and I should talk to him in the morning, but he didn't. Instead he swung his legs over the side of the bed, reached for his glasses, and got up. "Okay," he said, yawning, as he tied the belt of his robe, "let's go to my office."

Once we were both seated, him in his chair and me across from him, he clasped his hands and leaned forward. But he didn't speak.

Obviously he wasn't going to give me any help, so I sucked in a deep breath and exhaled. Then I got right to the point. "I injected testosterone."

He nodded and didn't say anything. His silence was worse than a lecture. He looked at his hands and twiddled his thumbs. Finally he looked up and asked, "Why?"

"I dunno." I shrugged. "I really want a scholarship."

"Are you still injecting?"

"No."

"How much did you do?"

"Not even one cycle. Like five weeks, maybe."

He put his elbows on the table and buried his head in his hands. Just looking at the top of his head, his lowered head, made me feel ill. "I'm so sorry, Dad. I really am. I just wanted it so badly."

Dad lifted his head. "Why would you take a steroid and jeopardize all you've worked for?"

"I guess I thought I had to."

"You *didn't* have to, Nathan. You're good enough." He sat back. "I think I knew you were up to something. But I kept telling myself it could be natural growth. But then the other day in the kitchen, I figured something was very wrong."

"What am I gonna do?" I asked softly.

"What do you think you should do?"

"I'm not injecting anymore. And I'll never do it again."

My dad leaned back in his chair, removed his glasses, and rubbed his forehead. "That's the first step."

Dad put his glasses back on and stared into space, obviously thinking, so I just remained quiet. Time ticked by. I stayed quiet and waited. Would my lacrosse career be over? Would he make me quit?

Finally Dad looked at me, his eyes red-rimmed. "I've watched you play lacrosse since you were five years old. I'd never seen such passion and drive in a child. No matter how small you were, you just kept going. Guys would hit you and you'd fall and bounce right back up. You would get injured and never say a word. You were always up early if you had practice and we never had to force you to go, ever. You always wanted to be there and you were always the first kid on the field. I don't understand why you did what you did. And I don't condone it."

"I know what I did was wrong."

Dad chewed the side of his mouth for a second. Was he going to drop the bomb that he wanted me to fess up to everyone? If he did, I would. And that would be the end of my scholarship hopes, but at least I would have been honest.

"I'll tell everyone the truth," I said.

My dad made direct eye contact with me. "I think you deserve a second chance, Nathan, because of the hard work you've put into your sport. But it will come with stipulations. You tell me you've stopped injecting, and I believe you. Now I'll do some research on the post-cycle therapy and I'll help you with that. Don't inject another thing into yourself. I will do random urine tests on you for the next few months. When you're clean, we'll talk."

"I'll do the random tests, Dad. I promise. Anytime you ask."

"You won't have a choice."

"I have to tell Derkie," I said. "Blackie knows, I'm sure. He's figured it out."

"I'm not proud of you for what you've done, Nathan, but I'm proud of you for handling this so maturely and confessing and stopping it before it's too late. And I think it's a good idea to talk to your coach."

"Are you going to tell Mom?"

My dad sighed and ran his hand through his hair. "Good question." He pursed his lips for a second, then said, "We're a team, so yes, I'll tell her."

I hung my head. "She'll be so disappointed."

"You've made a mistake and you've admitted it. She'll be fine."

"I'll have lost her trust."

"Trust is earned. I think it might take some time to get ours back. But you will."

"Okay."

"This isn't just about Mom and me. You have to trust yourself too. You have what it takes to succeed in your sport, especially the passion." My dad gestured with his hands at the word *passion*. "You don't need anything artificial. Don't give up on yourself so easily. The thing is, Nathan, if you were to get a scholarship while on testosterone, it would be like cheating on an exam, and you wouldn't have pride in your success."

I bit my bottom lip to keep my emotions under control. Of course he was right. When Derkie complimented my game, I didn't feel good about it. I didn't want a scholarship because I'd cheated. I wanted a scholarship because I was good, because I deserved it.

"I'm here to help you," Dad said, "but only because I've seen how hard you've worked over the years. Yes, it goes against my grain but . . . everyone deserves a second chance." He got to his feet. "I'm going back to bed."

I got to my feet too. Dad put his hand on my shoulder. "I believe in you, son. I may not always show it, but I always have."

"Thanks, Dad." I could barely get the words out of my mouth.

"Come here." He pulled me into his body and gave me a huge hug.

And that's when I broke down.

CHAPTER THIRTEEN

When I woke up, it was 11:00 a.m. I must have fallen asleep right after my talk with my dad. As usual, I picked up my phone to check my texts. News of the accident had obviously circulated because I had a ton of texts asking me how I was, but not one was from Allie.

But there was one from Derkie and he wanted me to call him. Closing my eyes, I pressed my fingers to my temples and breathed slowly in and out. This was one call I had to make and definitely my first call. After three rings Derkie answered and said, "Nathan." He sounded out of breath.

"Hey," I said back.

"How are you doing?"

"I'm okay. I have a cracked rib."

"I've heard you're darn lucky, kid. What's the prognosis on the rib?"

"Hopefully, not long," I replied, aware that I was probably going to be out for at least four weeks, which really sucked. Especially since I couldn't lift. All my muscle would be lost and this could really set be back. But I would get back to the gym as soon as I was healthy and I would stay clean. I had to.

"I know it's Saturday, but I want to come see you today. Before practice."

"Sure, come to my office. I'll be here."

Derkie's office door was open when I arrived and he was sitting at his desk, talking on his phone. When he saw me, he waved me to sit down. He ended his call within seconds and set his phone down.

"So, quite a scare you had."

"I'm okay." I tried not to wince when I sat down.

"I've talked to Blackie." He glanced at the clock on his wall. "He's coming to see me in thirty. He phoned and said he wanted to talk to me about you."

I nodded. I knew exactly what Blackie wanted to talk to Derkie about. Blackie knew. I had to talk now. I wanted Derkie to hear what I'd done from me. I sucked in a deep breath before I said, "I have something else to tell you."

"Okay," said Derkie.

My heart raced. Sweat beaded on my upper lip. "I, um, injected testosterone. But I've stopped. I didn't even do one cycle."

Derkie sat back in his chair and sighed. Disappointment seemed to carve its way into every line on his face. I hung my head.

"Recently?"

"Yes," I whispered.

"So that's the weight gain."

"Yeah." I looked up, made eye contact, and nodded.

"Why, Nathan?" He used his hands to talk.

"I thought I needed to be big to get a scholarship."

He shook his head, as if he was exasperated. "You will get a scholarship because you're good. You're going to fill out. And you have skill and grit and determination. You didn't need to go to such extreme measures." He paused. Then he leaned forward. "Nathan, your lacrosse career is not a sprint. If you don't get your scholarship this year, keep playing and you might get it the year after. This injury might set you back a bit. I will help you in any way I can but . . ." He squinted. "You're *definitely* not injecting anymore?"

"Definitely."

"I won't help you if you are. And as much as I like you, if I ever hear you're back on the juice, I'll be forced to deal with the issue, and your chances of a scholarship will be gone for good."

"I'll never inject again," I said. I proceeded to tell him the entire story, leaving out a few parts like where I got the steroid, but I did tell him all about my dad and how he was going to make me do random urine tests.

When I was finished, Derkie sat silent for a few seconds before he looked at me and said, "I believe you. But more than that, Nathan, I believe *in* you. You're a good kid and, like your father, I'm going to give you a second chance. But also like your father, I think there should be consequences. I'm going to take your C away."

"Okay," I said. I hung my head. I liked being the captain and it had been such an honour to be chosen by Derkie. I felt sick to my stomach at being stripped of the letter, but I deserved it.

"I also would like you to go see a sports psychologist to

work through why you felt you needed to take such drastic measures to reach your goal," said Derkie.

"Sure," I replied. "I'll do that."

"I'm also going to call your parents and discuss these random tests. I want to be involved and be informed about all results. Normally I would make you do a urine test with a doctor, but since your father, who *is* a doctor, is going to take care of that, it won't be necessary. We'll work as a team to get you through this."

"Will you involve Blackie?"

"Good question."

"I think he might have figured it out," I said. "I bet that's why he asked to meet you today about me."

"Good thing you got here first," said Derkie. "Shows character. I think Blackie can be a help here."

"Okay," I said. "I really appreciate you not kicking me off the team. I know I was wrong. I do. I just want this so badly."

"Did you feel good about the extra muscle? And how you played?"

I shook my head. "No. Not at all. It felt like cheating, and it was."

That night, after not receiving one text from Allie all day, I decided to give her a call.

"Hey," she said softly.

"How are you doing?" I asked.

"I'm okay. My head still hurts and my knee is swollen."

"Can I come by?"

"Sure, if you want to. You can't stay long though."

Silence.

Finally I said, "That's okay. I just want to see you."

When I told my parents I was going to see Allie and I was taking the C-Train, my mother immediately said she would drive me over. I felt like a little kid sitting in the passenger side, having my mother drive me. And it would be like this for three long months.

"Can we stop at a grocery store?" I asked. "I want to get Allie some flowers."

My mom took her eyes off the road for a second to glance at me. "You're not doing any other drugs, are you?"

"No, Mom, I'm not."

"Good. Keep it that way."

"I will." By the way she asked the question, I knew I was in for a couple of months of her checking my room out. I was going to have to earn her trust back.

"Everyone makes mistakes, Nathan," she said in a very serious tone. "Owning up like you did took courage, and I'm proud of you for how you're handling it now."

"I'll never do it again," I replied. "No matter what happens. Even if I don't get a scholarship this year."

"If you're supposed to get a scholarship, you will. And if not, something else will come for you." She cranked the wheel and drove into the supermarket parking lot. "I'm sure they'll have nice bouquets of daisies." She gave me a little smile. "Such sunny flowers might cheer her up. Maybe see if you can get a bunch in a vase."

In the supermarket I bought a bouquet of some yellow, orange, and white flowers already in a glass vase, along with a bag of Oreos. Oreos were Allie's favourite cookie.

My ribs hurt with every breath I took, reminding me of the accident and what I had done to Allie. I got back in the car and Mom drove off. She tried to talk to me about Allie, but since I didn't know what was going to happen between us, I didn't allow the discussion to go too far.

When Mom pulled up in front of Allie's, I said, "Thanks for the lift."

"How long will you be?"

"I'll text you," I said.

Allie lived with a professional couple who had no children and kept their house looking like the cover of a home-and-garden magazine. When I knocked, Abigail, Allie's billet mom, opened the door. Today Abigail wasn't dressed in one of her power suits. Instead she wore a track suit, her lounging wear, I figured.

"Is Allie expecting you?"

"Yeah," I answered. I sensed some animosity.

"You really banged her up," she stated.

"I know."

I slipped out of my shoes and tried to line them up perfectly, because I knew that was a pet peeve of Abigail's. She looked down and nodded her head in approval. Then I walked to Allie's room. I rapped softly on the door.

"Come in," she said.

I opened her door and saw her lying on the bed with her leg on a pillow. Her knee looked painfully swollen and my heart dropped to the ends of my big toes. I had done this to her. I held out the flowers and the cookies. "Here," I said.

She gave me a little smile. "Thanks." She took the flowers and Oreos and put them on the night table.

I sat on the end of her bed and ran my hands up and down my jean-clad thighs. All the words I had planned to say got caught in my throat, so I blurted out, "I'm so sorry. I feel awful that I've done this to you."

"I think we should take a break," she said.

My mouth went dry and my heart felt really heavy, like it had been coated in mud. "I understand. It was my fault."

"It's not just the accident," she said softly. "I've got some things I need to work out."

"Yeah, me too." I lowered my head. A part of me wanted to tell her about the testosterone, unload, get it out, but another part of me knew she had enough to deal with, and now was definitely not the right time. Anyway, the words probably wouldn't come out right. There was no way Allie would understand why I'd injected. She was a purist. Besides, once Allie knew, it might leak out to other athletes. If it got to Carrie and then Aaron, the entire school would know. That would be so humiliating, plus I would give lacrosse a bad name. I didn't want to do that to my teammates. Our team had been through enough

"I'm not ready for some things yet," she said. "I don't know why. I'm sorry, Nathan. The accident just made me realize that you and I need a break."

I took her hand in mine and looked into her beautiful sad eyes.

"Maybe we can be friends," she whispered.

I felt tears creeping behind my eyelids, and I didn't want to cry in front of her. "That might be hard," I said. "I like you too much."

She pulled her hand from mine and looked away.

I sat up tall and tried to push my emotions aside. I wasn't very successful, so I lowered my head and said, "I have things to work on too. School, and of course my lacrosse."

"And me my basketball and healing this knee."

I pulled out my phone, held it up, and tried to joke. "I have to rely on my mother to pick me up and take me home for three months."

The low chuckle that came from Allie's throat sounded great. Then she really started laughing and I did too, although I had to stop and grab my rib cage. "Ouch," I said. "That hurts."

She put her hand over her mouth to stifle her laughter. Then I leaned over and pressed my forehead against hers. "I'll miss you," I said.

"I'll miss you too." Her breath misted in front of my face, warming it. I wanted to kiss her but instead I pulled back.

My phone beeped.

"I gotta go," I said.

"See you at school," she said.

As I waited outside for my mother, I thought about everything that had happened. Allie and I had just split up and my heart was aching. So weird. I'd never felt this kind of feeling before, but now I guess I could say I knew what a broken heart was.

Maybe if I put all my energy into my lacrosse, in time all the bad feelings would go away. To see Allie at school, hobbling around on crutches, would be painful. I knew that for certain.

I wanted to fight for her, like I wanted to fight to make Derkie give me back the C — and fight to regain my family's trust.

Sometimes good old hard work pays off.

I had goals and I was going to reach them the right way.

The honest way.

ACKNOWLEDGEMENTS

Publishing a book takes a team. I write about fictional sports teams, but in real life, I work with a terrific team at James Lorimer and Company. Carrie Gleason is the best editor and keeps me organized and on track. The design team makes amazing books and the most wonderful covers. The promotions team helps get news of the book out to the public. And head coach, Jim Lorimer, is always there to support the project. For this book, I also relied on a lot of outside help. Thanks to Dr. Mark Aubry, Glenn Kulka, and my brother, Dr. John Schultz; they all answered my questions about steroids. Ken Weipert, principal of the National Sport School (a real sports school), endorsed the series, and Quinn Hamilton helped with my lacrosse questions. And, of course, as always, I have to say thanks to you, my lovely readers, for reading the stories I write.

ABOUT LORNA SCHULTZ NICHOLSON

One Cycle is Lorna Schultz Nicholson's eleventh novel and the third book in her Podium Sports Academy series. Lorna is also the author of seven non-fiction books and two picture books about hockey. Growing up in St. Catharines, Ontario, Lorna played volleyball, basketball, soccer, softball, and hockey, and was also a member of the Canadian National Rowing Team. She attended the University of Victoria, British Columbia, where she obtained a Bachelor of Science Degree in Human Performance. From there Lorna worked in recreation centres, health clubs, and as a rowing coach until she turned her attention to writing. Today Lorna works as a full-time writer and does numerous school and library visits throughout the year to talk about her books. She divides her time between Calgary, Alberta, and Penticton, British Columbia, and lives with her husband, Hockey Canada President Bob Nicholson, her son, who plays junior hockey, and various hockey players who billet at their home for several months of the year. She also has two daughters who now live away from home, but thankfully, the two family dogs keep her company while she writes.

"Lorna's books are a great read for kids and their parents. They really help teach the importance of having good values both in hockey and in life."

— Wayne Gretzky

"Podium Sports Academy gives readers a look into the life of a student-athlete. Through Lorna's books, we have an opportunity to develop an appreciation for the commitment and dedication necessary to maintain the delicate balance associated with being a teenager, athlete, and student."

— Ken Weipert, Principal, National Sport School, Calgary, AB

ROOKIE

> I hated this.
>
> I wanted the blindfold off and this to be over. I had a horrible feeling in my stomach. None of this was me. I just wanted to play hockey. *Stay tough,* I told myself. I tried to breathe.
>
> "Let's execute," spat Ramsey.

Aaron Wong is away from home, a hockey-star-in-the-making at Podium Sports Academy. He's special enough to have earned his place at a top school for teen athletes — but not special enough to avoid the problems of growing up.

Buy the books online at www.lorimer.ca

DON'T MISS THIS BOOK!

VEGAS TRYOUT

"It's Vegas. And Vegas is all about how you look.

"You need to lose at least ten pounds." Coach snapped her book shut. "This had better change by next weigh-in. You're the shortest girl on this team and now you're the heaviest."

Lap after lap, I swam as hard as I could to get my frustration out.

Suck it up and swim, Carrie."

Synchro swimmer Carrie doesn't have the body shape that most athletes in her sport have, so when her coach takes her off the lift and puts her on a special diet, Carrie takes it too far.

Buy the books online at www.lorimer.ca